Chapter One

My heart is thumping so fast, I feel like it wants to jump right out of my chest. My shoulder muscles are aching and my hands burn as they pull the oars. Behind me, I can hear Jim counting the strokes – two hundred and ten, two hundred and eleven ... As I lean backwards on each stroke, I can sense my ponytail brushing the floor of the boat – swish, swish, swish. The boat is rocking like crazy, and I wonder if I'm going to be thrown out. A sudden rush of ice-cold water hits me in the face, and drips down my cheeks, but I don't even blink. I have to keep going, no matter what. A small silvery fish flies past my face, just missing my nose. I want to give up, but I can hear Beth's voice from what feels like a million miles away.

'Keep going, Molly. You can do it. Don't stop now – you can't let the team down. We're almost there.'

5

It seems like a million years have passed before I hear the most beautiful sound in the world – the bell announcing the end of the race. I let go of the oars, and before I have time to check my hands for blisters, Beth is hugging me.

'We did it!' she shrieks. 'We did it!'

My legs are a bit wobbly as I climb out of the boat so I quickly sit down on the grass next to the washing line. Mum hands me a glass of water.

'Well done, darling,' she says. 'All you needed were three hundred strokes in your ten minutes, and you even went over that! You and Beth have beaten Jim and me in the Saturday challenge – again!'

* * *

I don't know what it feels like to row the whole way across the Atlantic, but I wonder if it feels a bit like this?

Even though I was rowing a battered old dinghy

that Jim found in a skip somewhere.

Even though the boat was on the grass, and Mum had been rocking it from side to side while I rowed.

Even though the spray of water came from the garden hose that Jim was holding.

Even though the only fish in the garden came from an old fishing game Beth had found in the shed.

Even though the finishing bell was a saucepan and a wooden spoon.

Beth was dancing around the garden, singing 'We are the champions.' Mum and Jim were laughing like little kids. I lay back on the grass and tried to catch my breath.

My best friend Beth and her dad moved in with Mum and me ages ago. At first that was really weird, but now I was getting used to it, and sometimes I can hardly remember a time when they didn't live with us. Like all dads, Jim can be a bit annoying sometimes, but he comes up with the craziest and best ideas. The Saturday challenge was in its third week, and it was

always Mum and Jim against Beth and me. The rules were a bit vague, but no one cared – mostly we were all too busy laughing for anything else to matter.

The first week, Jim set up a very complicated obstacle course in the garden, where you had to run the first half in odd wellies, and the second half with a glass of water in your pocket. The second week, we all had to pretend to be horses, jumping over bamboo canes propped up on kitchen chairs, with extra points for the best horsey sound effects. These things might sound a bit lame and stupid, but as long as you know there's no one planning to make a video and post it on YouTube, they are really, really fun.

After a while, everyone calmed down.

'That was so brilliant, Jim,' I said. 'I think that was the best challenge ever.'

'Thanks, Molly,' he said. 'I do my best – and wait till you see what I've got planned for next week.'

'Tell us, please, Dad!' said Beth. 'I don't think I can wait a whole week to find out.'

'Sorry, sweetie-pie,' he said as he put his arm around her. 'You're just going to have to be patient. Now let's go inside, I think it's time we ordered that takeaway you've been promised. How about we get a big pot of Irish stew?'

'Noooo,' I wailed. 'I hate Irish stew more than anything in the world – except for maybe bacon and cabbage.'

Jim laughed. 'I know, Molly,' he said. 'I'm just winding you up. How about we all get pizza?'

* * *

Much later, Beth and I were lying on her bed and she was telling me about the maths project she's starting.

'It's going to be so cool,' she said. 'It's all about pie charts.'

'So, like apple pie and cherry pie and stuff?'

She rolled her eyes. 'You *do* know that pie charts are a way of representing categorical data in a circular

9

form?'

'Er ... I might have heard Mrs Gallagher going on about something like that,' I said. 'But even thinking about it gave me a headache so I stopped listening.'

'Sorry, Moll,' she said. 'But you know you're going to have to do an exam on pie charts in a few weeks' time, don't you?'

'I guess I'm hoping that if I don't think about it, it won't happen.'

'That's your best plan?'

'Oh, Beth,' I said. 'It's easy for you – you're so good at maths, but even when I try I'm ...'

'Hold it right there,' she said. 'It's time we did something about this.'

She jumped off the bed, and pulled a notebook and some coloured pencils out of her bedside locker. Then she sat down next to me again.

OK,' she said. 'Imagine there are twenty kids in the class, and we asked them each what their favourite pie was. And if five of them say they like rhubarb pie,

and four of them like blueberry pie and ...'

And for the next twenty minutes Beth wrote down stuff and drew stuff and it was like a miracle. For the first time ever, maths didn't just make sense, it actually seemed easy.

'Oh, Beth,' I said. 'I can't believe it. I actually get it. I actually *get* maths. You've worked a miracle.'

She smiled. 'And you can use pie charts in all kinds of ways. If you wanted to show how many people like different pets you could ...'

'But then it would be called a pet chart, right – because a pie chart is just about pies?'

For a second she looked so disappointed in me, and then I laughed, and she punched my arm and she laughed too.

'Hey,' I said then. 'Your dad has loads of pie charts on the wall of his office. I never understood them before – they were just like not very pretty wallpaper, but now.....'

'Well, the charts in Dad's office are kind of boring,'

she said. 'They're all about profits and loss and sales targets and lame stuff like that, but maybe next time you're there you can ...'

'We're going to be in your dad's office next week,' I said. 'Isn't that when the office family party is on?'

Beth's face went red and for a second, she didn't answer. Beth and I are almost like sisters, which is really great – and it means that I know what she's saying, even when she hasn't opened her mouth.

'Beth?'

'Oh,' she said. 'About Dad's office party ...'

Chapter Two

'Bye, Molly darling,' said Mum. 'We'll be back before ten – but I have my phone if there's an emergency.'

I could feel stupid tears coming to my eyes. *This* was an emergency. I couldn't believe Mum and Jim and Beth were all going to Jim's work party without me.

Beth hugged me. 'I'm so sorry about this,' she said. 'I wish you could come with us, Molly.'

She didn't look very sorry, though. She almost looked like she was trying not to smile. Now I really wanted to cry. What was going on? Was Beth getting fed up of me? Was she actually glad to have a few hours away from me? She's supposed to be my very best friend, and ...

'I'm sorry too,' said Jim. 'But for some reason,

tickets were very hard to get this year. I was really lucky to even get three.'

I'm not even sure why I was so upset. Jim's work has parties every month or two and most of them are pretty lame. His boss's kids are totally weird, and the food always tastes like salty cardboard. Mostly Beth and I beg to go home long before the end.

Maybe it was the thought of being left out that hurt the most. The four of us do everything together these days, and I *so* didn't like the idea of the others doing something that didn't include me.

I guess Jim and Beth had to go to the party so he can get promoted or something, but why couldn't Mum just skip it and stay home with me?

Why couldn't we let the others go off together, so Mum and I could snuggle up on the couch and watch movies together the way we used to when it was just the two of us?

Why ...?

'Actually, Jim,' said Mum then. 'I've just had a

thought.' For a second I felt hopeful – maybe Mum was reading my mind – she's usually quite good at that. But then she continued. 'Maybe we should walk to the party instead of driving? It'll be very hard to find a parking space at this time of the evening.'

Then they had a big talk about whether to drive or walk or get the bus and I felt like screaming at them. *At least you're going somewhere! I'll be stuck here all on my own and it so isn't cool.*

But as they put on their coats, it was almost like they'd forgotten I even existed. Their excited smiles were driving me crazy – couldn't they at least *pretend* to be sad about leaving me on my own?

'I'll be perfectly fine,' I said. 'Don't any of you worry about me for a single second. I'll probably even have more fun here at home watching TV. You'll all be so ...'

Mum gave me her best death stare and I knew it was time to stop talking.

Then she kissed me on the forehead, and the three

of them set off for their big night out.

* * *

Half an hour later I was sitting on the couch drinking hot chocolate and eating the expensive biscuits Mum had hidden in her 'top secret' hiding place in the piano stool. I was just settling down to a movie, when my phone rang.

'Hi, Mollikins. How's my precious girl?'

'Dad!!!'

'That's me.'

Dad went to live in Africa years ago. Sometimes I'm still a bit mad at him for leaving, but mostly I really, really miss him. 'You haven't called for soooo long,' I said. 'I thought you'd forgotten all about your favourite daughter.'

I was in a bad mood, so I was giving him a hard time. We'd had a long chat the day before, so it was kind of weird that he was calling again. I usually only

talk to him once a week.

Dad laughed. 'I haven't forgotten about my only daughter,' he said. 'You know well that we spoke yesterday, Molly. Anyway, how are you tonight?'

'Mum and Jim and Beth have gone out without me,' I said. 'So how do you think I feel? I'm all on my own and I'm so lonely. They've gone to a party and they're going to be gone for hours and hours. I think they're going for pizza afterwards, and ice cream, and Jim said something about stopping off at the bowling alley too.'

OK, so I might have been exaggerating a small bit, but still, Dad didn't sound like he cared.

'Oh, well,' he said. 'I suppose you'd better just make the best of it – you should be glad the others are having a nice time.'

Suddenly I felt like crying again. He's my dad. He's supposed to be on my side – no matter what. Why wasn't he agreeing with me about how mean everyone was being? Why was I starting to feel like every-

one hated me?

Just then the doorbell rang.

'Hang on a sec, Dad,' I said. 'There's someone at the door.'

'So some randomer at the door is more important than your dear old dad?' he said as I went out into the hall. 'I remember a time when ...'

'Shhh, Dad,' I said. 'I need to see who it is.'

Mum has warned me a million times about opening the door when I'm on my own, so I stood on tiptoes to look through the spy-hole. There was a man standing on the doorstep, and for a second I felt a small bit afraid. I wasn't supposed to answer the door to a stranger – but what if he'd heard my footsteps? What if he knew I was there? What if he was planning to break in?

The man was on the phone, and suddenly he turned around so I could see his face.

He was smiling.

I knew that face.

I knew that smile.

'OMG!' I whispered.

I pulled off the chain, opened the door, and threw myself into his arms.

'Dad!' I said. 'What on earth are you doing here?'

* * *

We hugged for a long time. Whenever Dad tried to step back, I just held on tighter. I'd been waiting ages and ages for that cuddle, and I wasn't letting go that easily.

In the end, when my neck was stiff and my arms were hurting, I pulled away.

'Dad,' I said again. 'What are you doing here? How long are you staying? Why didn't you tell me you were coming? Why did ...?'

'Maybe I could come inside so we can talk?' he said.

'Er, I'm not sure about ... you see, Dad, the thing is ... maybe ...'

Now I felt really weird. Once upon a time this was Dad's home, but he didn't live here anymore. He hadn't lived here since I was eight years old. He'd come home from Africa to see me a few times before, but Mum was still mad at him then, so I had to meet him in a hotel, and he never came to the house.

Lots of stuff had changed since the last time I saw Dad. Now Jim lived in this house with Mum and me – and Beth. Now everything was different and I had a whole new life. I love my dad, and sometimes I wished things could be like they used to be, but I don't believe in fairytales anymore. I'm smart enough to know that I can't turn the clock back so Mum and Dad and I can live happily ever after.

And now Dad was standing on the doorstep of his used-to-be home, and things were totally awkward.

What if Mum and Jim came home?

What were they going to say when they saw Dad?

Was there going to be a big fight?

Were the police going to get involved?

No one likes the idea of their parents living thousands of miles away from each other, but I was sort of getting used to it. If Mum or Dad ended up in jail that would be a whole different story.

'Molly?'

'I'm sorry, Dad,' I said. 'This is too hard for me. I don't know what to say. I don't know what to do.'

Now he looked really sad. 'This was supposed to be a wonderful surprise for you,' he said. 'I thought you'd be happy to see me.'

'I *am* happy to see you. But you don't get how scary this is for me.'

'Sorry, Mollikins,' he said. 'Maybe we didn't think this out so well.'

'We?' I said, suddenly starting to figure out what was going on. 'Who's we? Who's been thinking stuff out without me? Did Mum and Jim and Beth know?'

'Yes,' said Dad. 'They all knew I was coming back, and we thought it would be nice to surprise you.'

'So I could've gone to Jim's party? That whole story

about there not being enough tickets was ...'

'Yes,' said Dad. 'Jim could have easily got you a ticket, but we all thought ...'

So that's why Mum and Jim and Beth were all grinning like crazy people when they left. I could feel angry tears coming to my eyes. I didn't care about Jim's stupid party, but I hate when people do things behind my back.

Dad put his arm around me. 'I'm sorry, my darling,' he said. 'None of this is your fault, but I know that what happened between your mum and me has been hard for you. Maybe I was being selfish when I came up with this idea, but all I wanted was to spend a few special hours with my little girl. After being away for so long, I wanted to have you all to myself. That's not so bad, is it?'

And I could've stayed angry. I could've given him a hard time – but it was so totally amazing having my dad back, I forgot about everything else and hugged him again.

'It's really great to see you,' I said. 'Now you'd better come inside. My hot chocolate's going cold.'

*　*　*

After the first few minutes, it was almost like he'd never been away. We chatted about his travels and my school, and my friends, and hockey and lots of stupid stuff.

It took me ages to get to the question I really wanted to ask him. Whenever Dad came home before, he only stayed for a few days. I was just getting used to him being there, and then I had to get used to him not being there all over again. Sometimes I wondered if it was even worth it. I wondered if there was a way of measuring these things. Could you weigh out all the happiness I had when Dad was home, and balance it against how much I cried when he left?

'Er, Dad,' I said in the end. 'How long are you stay-

ing? When do you have to get back to Africa? Can you stay for more than a few days this time?'

'I thought you'd never ask,' he said. 'I'm not going back.'

'How do you mean?'

'I've given up my job in Africa, and I start a new one here on Monday – so I'll be hanging around annoying you for a very long time.'

'That's so cool,' I said, as I hugged him again. 'It's really great, but ...'

Did he think he could act like the last few years had never happened?

Did he think he could step back into the life he'd walked away from?

'It's OK, Molly,' he said. 'I've read the books and seen the movies. I understand that you and your mum have moved on. I know things are going to be different, but I think it'll all be fine. I've booked into a bed and breakfast for a few nights, until I can find myself a new home.'

'So you're actually staying?' I said. 'You're really and truly staying?'

'Yup,' he said. 'Like it or not, you're going to be seeing a whole lot more of me from now on.'

And I jumped up and hugged him until he begged for mercy.

*　*　*

It was late when the others got back, but it felt like only a few minutes had passed.

Dad stood up when he heard Mum's key in the front door and I couldn't help feeling nervous.

I remembered how crazy Mum went when Dad left. Was she going to be mad at him all over again?

Dad had left his coat thrown on the sofa – was Mum going to cut it into tiny pieces with her sharpest scissors? Was she going to crochet it into an ugly, scratchy blanket? Should I warn him?

Or would that just remind him about what had

happened before?

Was he going to give Mum a hard time for cutting up his DVDs and his ties and loads of his other stuff?

And what were Jim and Beth supposed to do while my family tried to figure out how to survive this strange situation?

Was this all going to be totally weird and embarrassing?

But then Mum and Jim and Beth were in the room. Mum and Dad hugged each other, and Dad and Jim shook hands.

Beth jumped up and down and said, 'Wasn't that the coolest surprise ever, Molly? Did you really have no clue? I thought I'd die, I wanted to tell you so badly.'

And I hugged her, and we all had a cup of tea, and everything was fine.

Chapter Three

a few weeks later, Beth and I crossed our fingers as we stared at Mum and Jim.

'Please, please, please,' said Beth. 'Clemmie always has the coolest parties, and it's the first time she's ever invited us ...'

'And we'll be really good, we promise,' I said.

Mum looked at Jim. 'What do you think?' she said. 'Should we let them go?'

'I'm OK with it if you're OK with it,' he said.

Mum nodded. 'Then it's a "yes" from us.'

'Yesss!' said Beth. 'We're going to a party! Come on, Molly. Let's go plan what to wear.'

* * *

Later on I called over to my dad's place. Dad was all

settled into his new flat and his new job, and I was slowly getting used to having him in my life again. It was kind of weird being able to see him any time I wanted, instead of waiting days and days for him to call me. Mostly that was good, but sometimes it was a bit strange. Sometimes I didn't know what to say to him – when I didn't have to squash it all into a single phone call.

'So what's happening, Mollikins?' he asked. 'Any exciting news from your world?'

'Actually there is,' I said. 'Beth and I have been invited to the coolest sleepover party in our friend Clemmie's house. Loads of the girls from hockey are going. Clemmie's mum said we can make a fire in the back garden and toast marshmallows, and there's these really cool things called s'mores and she said—

'Hang on a sec,' said Dad. 'Who's this girl? How come she's having this party at such short notice? Do we know her parents? Are they responsible people? Has your mum spoken to them?'

'Dad, stop fussing! And anyway, it's all sorted already. Mum and Jim said that Beth and I can go.'

'Last time I checked, Beth wasn't my daughter,' said Dad. 'And whether she's going or not isn't any of my business. I'm only worried about you.'

'Dad, you know I'm not a kid anymore, right?'

'But you'll always be my little—'

'Dad!'

'Well, anyway, I think your mum might have been a little bit hasty. One of us will have to talk to Clemmie's parents before we make a definite decision.'

'The decision has been made *already*, Dad. It's a done deal.'

'Not as far as I'm concerned. I want to know what kind of supervision there's going to be tomorrow night. Can you give me the phone number, please?'

'So you're actually going to call Clemmie's parents? You don't even know them.'

'That's exactly my point.'

'But if you call them you'll make me into the big-

gest loser in the world. Dad, how could you do that to me? No one else will be calling, so everyone will think I'm an idiot baby.'

'Or maybe they'll think that you're a girl with sensible parents who love her a lot.'

'Dad, you're being so pathetic right now. Actually I've changed my mind. If I can't go to the party without you turning me into a total loser, then I won't bother going.' I even forced out a little tear, to make him feel sorry for me, but it didn't work. He just shrugged.

'Suit yourself. It's your call. And I have to say that since you're acting like this, you probably aren't mature enough to go to the party, anyway. I think it's best if you tell this Clemmie girl that you can't go.'

'But, Dad—'

He gave me a look I was getting much too used to – the look that said that arguing wasn't going to help, and might even make things a whole lot worse. So I let myself out, and slammed the door behind me.

* * *

I ran all the way home and told Mum what had happened.

'But I can still go, can't I? You said—'

Mum gave a big, long sigh. 'I guess I should have asked your father before I said yes.'

'It's hardly your fault, Charlotte,' said Jim. 'In all fairness, you've been making the decisions, and that can't be expected to change overnight.'

'I know Eddie hasn't been around for a while,' said Mum. 'But he's still her father.'

'Being a father comes with responsibilities,' said Jim.

'I know that just as well as you do, but I still think we have to ...'

She stopped talking and looked at Jim, and then at me. Suddenly I understood that most of this conversation was going to happen when I wasn't in the room.

And in the end, I wasn't allowed to go to the party, and Jim changed his mind so Beth wasn't allowed to go either, and she didn't talk to me for a whole afternoon.

* * *

And that's kind of the way things continued. Mostly, it was totally cool having my dad around. Sometimes, though, Dad was totally annoying – like when he invited me over, and then acted surprised when Beth came too. Sometimes he didn't get that all the time he'd been away, Beth was the one I talked to, the one who made me feel better, the one who sort of made life OK. For a long time, Beth was a much bigger part of my life than he was.

One Sunday I told Dad about the Saturday Challenge we'd had the day before. Everyone had to swap shoes. It was a really funny story about Jim trying to run across the garden in a pair of Mum's sandals

– and I'm kind of OK at telling funny stories. Then I noticed that Dad wasn't laughing. He wasn't even smiling. He looked like he was trying not to cry, and at first I didn't get it, but then I realised that he was jealous. I stopped talking and put my arm around him. I was all mixed-up, though. Was I supposed to feel guilty for having fun?

But not everything was bad. Some of my visits to Dad were really great. Sometimes he told me stories about his time in Africa and he made me laugh so much I thought I was going to pee myself.

And sometimes, Dad made me so mad, I scared myself by wishing he'd just jump on a plane and fly back to Africa and never come home again.

* * *

'Let's go for burritos,' said Dad.

'Well, I'm not—'

'I know they're your favourites,' he said.

'How about we—?'

'My mind's made up,' said Dad. 'You deserve a treat. Come along, girls, you must be starving.'

It was a few weeks later, and Dad had asked Beth and me to go for lunch with him. We followed him into the restaurant and Beth and I went and sat at a table while Dad picked up the food.

'Now, girls,' he said when he came back with the tray. 'Eat up. I got extra-large burritos, because I know how much you both love them.'

When we'd finished eating, Beth and I went to wash the sticky sauce off our faces and fingers.

'Please, tell him, Molly,' she said as we went into the bathroom. 'I used to love burritos, but it's like your dad can't stop buying them for us. I think I'll die if I've got to eat another one in this lifetime.'

'If I live for ten lifetimes, I don't think I'll ever want to see a burrito again.'

'So tell him.'

'I'll tell him tomorrow,' I said. 'I promise.'

'That's what you said last week – and the week

before.'

'I know,' I said. 'And I'm sorry – it's just that I don't want to hurt his feelings. When he brought us here that first time, and we said we loved it, he was so happy, it was like we'd given him a present. After being away so long, I think knowing what I like seems to be a big deal for Dad.'

For a second I felt sad. There's so much Dad doesn't know about me. He doesn't know how much I hate Irish stew and love chocolate cake. He doesn't know what my favourite song is, or my favourite movie. Sometimes it scares me to think that Jim knows me better than my own dad does.

'I get what your dad's trying to do,' said Beth. 'And it's totally sweet. I know he's trying to be nice and everything, but things can't go on like this. I'm going to start looking like a burrito if he doesn't stop.'

I giggled. 'OK,' I said. 'I'll tell him we'd like to try some other food next time.'

When Beth and I came out of the bathroom, I

could see my dad at the other side of the restaurant. His head was down, and he looked really sad and alone.

'Hey, Dad,' I said, trying to sound cheerful. 'What are you doing for the rest of the weekend? Have you got any exciting plans?'

'Charlotte and my dad are taking Molly and me bowling tomorrow,' said Beth, not very helpfully. I kicked her, and luckily she got it at once. 'Well, they might take us bowling,' she said quickly. 'Or we might just stay at home – which would be totally boring.'

'Oh,' said Dad. 'I haven't got any real plans. I might just tidy up my flat and read the paper for a while.'

Now I felt sad. Beth and I had been in his flat earlier, and it was really tidy, and the paper was all crumpled like he'd read every single page a couple of times already.

'Why don't you go out and meet some of your friends, Dad?' I suggested.

He didn't answer at first, and as the seconds passed,

I realised that Dad didn't have any friends these days. Except for work and burrito-buying trips with Beth and me, he never seemed to go anywhere anymore.

'Oh, you know how it is,' he said. 'I've been gone for a long time, and people have drifted away. I'm sure I'll settle in soon, and then I can catch up with some of the old gang.'

As he said the words, I realised that back when he and Mum were together, they mostly hung out with her friends, who were now busy hanging out with Mum and Jim. Poor Dad had no one at all – except for me.

* * *

On the way back, Beth and I talked about the hockey match we'd played the day before, but Dad barely said anything.

'Beth got such a great goal,' I said, when we were nearly at Dad's flat. 'She's our best player and the other team had no clue how to stop her.'

'Molly's a great player too,' said Beth. 'She can tackle anyone.'

'I'd like to see that,' said Dad. 'Do you think I could come to your next game?'

Suddenly I realised that Dad had never once seen me play, and that made me feel really bad – for him and for me.

'Er, that might be a bit weird, Dad,' I said. 'Parents used to come to matches when we were eight or nine, but now ...'

'That's OK,' said Dad in a weird, sad voice. He sounded like a lost little kid. I felt sorry for him, and I also felt like shaking him. He was a grown-up, so why couldn't he get his act together and fix his own problems?

A man was walking past us, and I was getting ready to step behind Dad to make room on the path.

'Eddie?' said the man then. 'You're back? And Molly – I haven't seen you for so long I hardly recognized you. You've got so big.'

I rolled my eyes at Beth. Did adults go to a special school to learn to say those stupid things?

'Stephen,' said Dad. 'How are you?'

They started to talk, but it was polite talk, like when you're in the doctor's waiting room or something, or like you really want to move on, but don't know how. Stephen wasn't smiling – and neither was Dad.

Beth grabbed my arm. 'If we don't hurry we'll be late for hockey training,' she said.

'Oh,' I said. 'You're right. See you, Dad. See you, Stephen.'

'Bye, darling,' said Dad giving me a quick hug. 'I'll call you in a few days – maybe we can go for burritos?'

Behind his back, Beth looked like she was trying to stop herself from throwing up and I tried not to laugh.

'Er, maybe,' I said. 'Give us a call.'

'Who was that guy?' said Beth, as we headed home. 'Why didn't you introduce us?'

'Sorry,' I said. 'That was my dad's brother – my

Uncle Stephen. I guess you must have met him years ago, before Dad went to Africa.'

'Maybe, but I don't remember that. I didn't even remember that your dad had a brother. How come you never talk about him?'

'It's a bit awkward. Dad and Stephen don't get on very well,' I said.

'I could see that,' said Beth. 'Did they have a fight or something?'

'I have no clue. All I know is I've never seen them acting like brothers are supposed to. They haven't even met up since Dad got back from Africa. They only see each other by accident like they did just now, or at weddings and funerals and stuff – and then they act like talking to each other is some kind of torture or something.'

'That's so sad – especially now that ...'

She stopped talking, so I finished her sentence for her, '... now that dad doesn't have any friends.'

'Exactly,' said Beth. 'No offence, Molly, but it looks

to me like your dad could do with fixing his relation-ship with his brother. He's lonely. He needs someone to hang out with.'

'You're right, but …'

'We need to help him,' said Beth.

'How?'

'Sorry, Molly. I guess that's something we're going to have to figure out.'

Chapter Four

On the way home from hockey, Beth and I met Graham, who is Beth's dad's uncle. Most uncles are fairly sensible, but Graham isn't like most uncles. He acts like he's never read the 'how-to-be-boring' book for grown-ups. Graham's long hair was tied up in a bun and he was cycling on a bright pink bike with a huge straw basket on the front.

'Look what I've got,' he said as he stopped beside us.

I couldn't help feeling excited. Anything in Graham's basket was likely to be very interesting.

Beth and I watched as he pulled back the fluffy purple blanket.

'Oh,' said Beth. 'They are soooo adorable!'

She was right. Curled up inside the basket were four teeny-tiny ginger kittens.

I leaned in and touched one – it was soft and fluffy and warm. It opened its huge blue eyes and mewed softly.

'Oh, Graham,' I said. 'These are the sweetest things ever. Where did you get them? Are you going to keep them?'

He smiled. 'I got them in the animal shelter. Their mother died so they need someone to care for them for a few weeks – they have to be bottle-fed every couple of hours. I won't be keeping them after that, though – I travel too much, so it wouldn't be fair to have a pet.'

'So what's going to happen them?' asked Beth.

'Well, hopefully the animal shelter will be able to find forever homes for them,' said Graham.

Beth looked at me. 'Are you thinking what I'm thinking?'

'I'm not sure,' I said. 'What are you thinking?'

'I'm thinking maybe your dad would like one of these kittens,' she said. 'His flat wouldn't seem so

empty if he had a cute little kitty living with him – and you and I could be like the cat's big sisters – or something.'

'That's *exactly* what I was thinking,' I said. 'Could we have one of these babies for my dad, Graham, please?'

'Well,' said Graham. 'I'm all for generous gestures, but a kitten is a big responsibility. I wonder how your dad would feel about that.'

'Actually, that's a good question,' said Beth. 'Does your dad even like cats, Molly?'

'He totally loves them,' I said. 'He goes all soppy when he sees a cat on TV, and he always pets strays when he sees them – even when they're crazy, spitty ones with scabby eyes and tangled-up fur.'

'That reminds me …' began Graham, and then I remembered too.

'That's how you and Jeanie became friends, wasn't it?' I said.

'Yeah,' said Beth. 'You two bonded over a spitty

kitten, didn't you?'

Graham nodded, and for a second I felt sad as I remembered his best friend Jeanie and our trip back to the 1960s to visit her.

Graham smiled, though. 'Happy days,' he said. 'But I need to get these kittens home for a feed, so about your dad, Molly?'

'If your dad loves cats so much,' said Beth, 'how come you never had one when he was living with you?'

'I'm not really sure,' I said. 'I remember begging for one when I was little, but nothing I said made any difference – Mum didn't mind, but Dad always said no.'

'Hmm,' said Graham. 'I think you and your dad need to have a long talk about this, Molly.'

'I guess,' I said, disappointed that our great idea didn't seem so great anymore.

Graham patted my shoulder. 'You're trying to be kind, which is always a good thing. And maybe your dad would love a little kitten – we just need to be sure

before you land on his doorstep with one, that's all.'

'I guess,' I said again.

'Let's take a picture to show your dad,' said Beth, taking out her phone. 'And if he wants a kitten he can choose the one he likes the best. I so love this little cutie with the white face.'

So Beth took a photo of the kittens, we said good-bye to Graham, and we headed back to Dad's place.

* * *

'Don't tell me you're hungry for more burritos!' said Dad when he opened the door of his flat.

Beth laughed a fake laugh. 'Not exactly.'

'We have a sort-of surprise,' I said.

'I have no idea what a sort-of surprise is,' said Dad. 'But I suppose it's got to be better than a sort-of dis-appointment. Why don't you come in and tell me what's going on?'

So Beth and I followed him into his very tidy flat.

Beth took out her phone, and waited for me to explain.

'We wanted to give you a surprise,' I said. 'But we're not really sure if you're going to like it.'

'So we brought a picture to show you first,' said Beth. 'And soon we'll be able to bring you the real thing – if you want us to.'

'And we really, really hope you will want us to,' I added.

Beth scrolled through her phone and handed it to Dad. I looked over his shoulder. 'Beth and I like the one with the white face, but it doesn't matter if he's not your favourite. The one with the white paws is very cute too – if you pick him you could call him Socks.'

'Or you could pick the one who's completely ginger,' said Beth. 'Basically they're all adorable, so we wouldn't mind which one you go for, would we Molly?'

'And Beth and I could come over and play with

him, couldn't we? And we could mind him for you if you're not here.'

Beth and I were so busy talking, it took me a minute to notice that Dad wasn't saying anything.

'So what do you think?' I asked. 'Aren't they the cutest little things you've ever, ever seen?'

Dad handed the phone back to Beth.

'Yes, Molly,' he said. 'I have to agree with you, they are very, very cute – almost irresistible.'

I hugged him. 'I knew you'd love them,' I said. 'And this flat will be so much nicer when it's got a pet living here. No offence, Dad, but it's a bit empty at the moment. Maybe you could even have two kittens. They'd be such fun and they could play together when you're out.'

Dad shook his head. 'You don't understand, darling,' he said. 'These kitties are totally adorable, but I'm afraid I won't be adopting one.'

'You're right,' I said, feeling angry. 'I *don't* understand. You live on your own, and you can do what you

want. You love cats, and these ones need a home, so I don't get why you won't take one. Please, Dad, please, please, please say you'll let us give you one.'

'No!' said Dad, sharply. 'Stop begging, Molly, because it's never going to happen.'

I wanted to argue more, but I could see that Dad had made up his mind, and Beth was looking embarrassed, so I knew I had to let it go.

'You're the boss,' I said sulkily. 'But you know you're making the biggest mistake of your life?'

Dad hugged me. 'I'm sad to say I've made lots of bigger mistakes than this,' he said. 'And I know you're trying to help me, sweetheart, but a cat – well, I'm afraid I'm never going to own a cat.'

'That's a weird thing to say,' I said, pulling away from him. 'How do you know you won't own a cat when you're an ancient old granddad? You could have one to keep your knees warm while you rock on your rocking chair all day long.'

Dad smiled a sad smile. 'I had a cat once,' he said.

'A very long time ago.'

I sat down next to him. 'You never said that before. Tell me about him. Was he cute like the ones on Beth's phone?'

'Pablo,' said Dad. 'He was called Pablo.'

'And what was Pablo like?' asked Beth.

'He was a tabby,' said Dad. 'With a beautiful grey and black coat and a white patch under his chin. He only had three legs, but—'

'Three legs!' I said. 'What happened?'

'I have no idea,' said Dad. 'He strayed into our house when I was a little boy, and his leg was already gone when he arrived.'

'Was he able to walk and stuff?' asked Beth.

'He could do pretty much anything any other cat could do,' said Dad. 'He could run and jump and climb. Stephen and I had a treehouse in the garden, and—'

'You had a treehouse!' I said. 'That's so cool.'

'It was very cool,' said Dad, smiling. 'Stephen and

I had a lot of fun in that treehouse when we were young lads. There was a ladder to get up and Pablo could scamper up there in a few seconds. He was a real little adventurer.'

'I don't get why I've never heard about Pablo before,' I said. 'And I've seen heaps of photographs of you and Uncle Stephen when you were little. How come Pablo isn't in any of them?'

'Pablo wasn't with us for very long,' said Dad. 'He ...'

'He what?' I asked. 'Did something terrible happen to him?'

Dad shook his head. 'Sorry, girls, but I don't want to talk about this anymore, if you don't mind. It's painful to me – and there's no sense dragging up unhappy memories for nothing.'

'You can tell us what happened,' I said. 'If you talk about it, maybe ...'

'No!'

Now I didn't know what to say. I felt a bit stupid for

thinking that one small kitten would be the answer to all of Dad's problems. And now I'd made him even sadder than before.

Dad got up. 'That was a very sweet thought, girls,' he said. 'Now you probably need to get going. Charlotte and Jim will be worried about you.'

'You're sure you're OK?' I asked.

He smiled. 'Everything's fine,' he said. 'Now off you two go, and have fun. See you soon.'

As Dad closed the door behind us, I tried not to cry. Why did life always have to be so complicated?

* * *

Later, when Beth went for a walk with her dad, I told Mum all about the kittens, and how Dad got upset when he heard we wanted to give him one, and about Pablo the mystery cat.

'That's so strange,' she said. 'In all the years I've known your dad, he never once mentioned having a cat. I used to talk a lot about the pets I had when

I was a girl and because your dad never joined in, I presumed he'd never had one.'

'I know you went out together when you were very young,' I said.

'Did I tell you that?'

I smiled. She'd never exactly told me, but when Beth and I went back to the 1980s we had learned a lot about my mum – she was a very scary teenager, she once thought that yellow dungarees were a good fashion choice, and she was going out with my dad when she was only fourteen!

'Anyway,' I said. 'I'd love to know more about Pablo. Did you know Dad when he was a little kid? Did he live near here?'

'No,' said Mum. 'When he was small, he lived at the other side of town – Castle Street, if I remember correctly. We didn't meet until we were in our teens, and ...'

'And what?'

'Your dad never liked to talk about his childhood –

it was like a forbidden zone between us.'

'That's weird. Do you think something terrible happened to him when he was a kid?'

She shook her head. 'I don't think so. After I married, I got to know his parents quite well – they died when you were a baby, remember?'

'What were they like?'

'Well, they were serious people. I get the sense that they were very strict with their boys.'

'So maybe—?'

'Don't jump to conclusions, Molly. Your grandparents were a bit old-fashioned, but they were nice people, and they never mentioned anything dramatic about your dad's childhood. Times were hard back then, and parents had to be stricter than they are now.'

'And what about Uncle Stephen – did he ever say anything about when they were kids?'

She shook her head again. 'Stephen is a bit like your dad – those two aren't great communicators, I'm afraid,' she said. 'Mind you, I never got to know your

dad's brother very well.'

'Why?'

'There was always a coolness between him and your dad. They seemed almost like strangers, which is unusual since they were the only two in the family. I've never really understood their relationship. I know my sister, Mary, and I used to fight like cat and dog when we were little, but at heart we were always the best of friends. Mary and I used to …'

I could see that this conversation was about to go way off track. Mum loves talking about the olden days. That used to drive me crazy, but ever since I learned how to travel back in time, I can understand her a bit better. Even though I'm only thirteen, I've been back in 1960, and 1969, and 1984. Now I get that the past is a real place — and if you were there, it never really leaves you. It sort of travels around in the back of your mind, changing the way you think about stuff.

'I love hearing about when you were little, Mum,' I

said. 'But now I'm kind of worried about Dad. Did you ever talk to him about his relationship with Stephen?'

'Many times, but whenever I brought it up, your dad just shut me down. In the end I stopped mentioning it. Maybe that was wrong of me. Maybe I should have asked more questions ... But I can't go back in time and change that, can I?'

Well, actually ...

'Before today, I hadn't seen Stephen for ages and ages,' I said, quickly changing the subject. 'It'd be nice if Dad could see him and hang out with him for a bit, don't you think?'

'I agree,' said Mum. 'Family is important, and those two need to fix whatever is going on between them. Knowing your dad, though, I don't see that happening any time soon. I think sorting those two out could well be impossible.'

'Oh, well,' I said, as the beginning of an idea popped into my head. 'Sometimes impossible things happen.'

Chapter Five

Next morning, I met Mum on the landing.

'You're up early, Molly,' she said. 'Are you planning something I don't know about? Should I be worried?'

'Why do you always have to think the worst about me?' I snapped. 'Maybe I'm just up early because I want to get the most out of the day, like you always go on and on about.'

Mum held up her hands. 'I was just making conversation,' she said. 'Forget I spoke.'

'Fine,' I said. 'I will.'

I headed for Beth's room, not sure why I felt so angry. Mum was thinking the worst, but on this occasion she was right. I was planning something, and there was no way I was letting her find out what it was.

* * *

'Go away, Molly,' said Beth. 'It's still the middle of the night – and we're not going bowling till this afternoon.'

'You've got to get up,' I said, pulling the duvet off her head. 'Before bowling, there's something you and I have to do.'

'Forget it,' said Beth, grabbing the duvet and pulling it over her head again. 'Nothing is more important than my beauty sleep.'

'Nothing at all?'

'Zero. Zilch. NOTHING!'

'How about if I said we need to go visit Rico's shop? How about—?'

I didn't have time to finish the sentence as Beth threw back the duvet and jumped out of bed.

'Why are you just standing there?' she said. 'Where are my socks, and—?'

'You don't even know why I want to go to Rico's.'

'I've got a pretty good idea – and anyway, I don't really care why. You're usually not a big fan of Rico's, so if you want to go, I want to go, and you can explain on the way. Now pass me my jeans.'

'Those are actually my jeans,' I said, picking them up from the floor and handing them to her.

She grinned. 'Stop arguing over minor details, Molly. Go get ready – we've got a journey to go on.'

I smiled. Beth used to be really sensible, and always thought hard about things before doing them, but she changed after we accidentally went back to 1984 and she met her mum. Nowadays she's more up for doing stuff – more ready to take a chance. Also, she talks about her mum more – and I feel special because I'm the one she has those conversations with. I guess it's good to know that you don't have to be the exact same person for your whole life.

* * *

'I'm guessing this is about your dad?' said Beth as we

headed towards town.

I nodded. 'I've been thinking about it all night. Dad's so sad and lonely and I really want to make things better for him.'

'I totally get that, but he's just back home after years of living so far away. Maybe all he needs is some time to settle down?'

'He's had weeks and weeks to settle down, but it's not working. Every day he just gets sadder, and then, yesterday, when I saw him with Stephen, it's like a lightbulb went on in my head.'

'Sounds painful,' said Beth.

I punched her on the arm. 'You know what I mean. I started to wonder about why Dad and Stephen don't get on.'

'But remember your dad said how they used to play in the treehouse together?' said Beth. 'He made it sound like they were best buddies back in the day.'

'I know – but things so aren't like that now – and then when Dad mentioned Pablo, he was too sad to

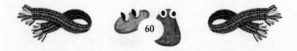

60

tell us the rest of the story.'

'You're right,' said Beth. 'All that was very weird. My hamster died when I was six, and I was really, really sad for ages – but in the end I got over it.'

'Exactly! We need to know what happened between Dad and Stephen – and why he can't talk about Pablo. Dad won't tell us, and Mum can't tell us.'

'So there's only one way to find out.'

* * *

We stopped outside Rico's shop. It looked just like before – kind of old and creepy – and the front door still needed painting.

'I know this thing was all my idea,' I said, feeling a bit scared. 'But maybe ...'

'You can't chicken out now,' said Beth. 'Your dad needs us.'

'Yeah, but we don't even know what we're looking for. We don't know when Dad and Stephen fell out

with each other, so we have no clue when we should go back to.'

'I'm not sure that even matters,' said Beth.

'What do you mean?'

'Well, we've time-travelled before – and it's not like getting on a train or a bus, is it? It's not like we can read a timetable and buy a ticket for … I don't know … say, 10 January 1922, and just go there. Usually we just concentrate on what we are trying to do, and it's always worked out.'

'So, you're saying we go through Rico's weird door and hope for the best?'

'I guess. Now let's get going – I don't want to be late for bowling.'

* * *

Rico was standing behind the counter, still polishing one of his sparky blue bottles. Just like before, he was wearing a suit and a snowy white shirt. Just like

before, he didn't seem surprised to see us. Just like before, I was terrified. Why couldn't the magic door have been guarded by a fluffy poodle instead if this creepy guy?

'Er, hi Rico,' said Beth. She was trying to sound brave, but I could tell by her voice that she was just as scared as I was. I guess time-travelling is never going to be as simple as running down to the shop to buy a loaf of bread.

'Hello, girls,' said Rico. 'So nice to see you again. Is there anything in particular I can do for you on this lovely day?'

It was actually raining outside, but I decided not to mention that. Maybe Rico was so weird that he thought rain was lovely. Maybe he was trapped in the shop forever, and had no clue what was going on outside. Maybe he'd been there for hundreds and hundreds of years, and Beth and I were the only people he ever saw.

'We'd like to use your back door,' I said. 'If that's OK?'

'Oh, that's always OK,' said Rico, smiling and showing us his perfect white teeth. 'You know the way.'

'Thanks,' said Beth and I together, and then I followed her through the velvet curtain.

We stood there for a second, getting used to the warm darkness, and the weird cinnamon smell. 'I used to like cinnamon,' I moaned. 'But now—'

'Sounds like how I feel about burritos,' said Beth.

I tried to punch her arm, but in the darkness I missed and my hand rubbed against something cold and squishy. I jumped and hit my head.

'Ouch! Let's get out of here,' I said. 'Before one of us gets killed.'

'OK,' said Beth. 'I'm good with that plan. Hold my hand and concentrate on your dad and Stephen and Pablo, the three-legged wonder cat.'

* * *

Even though I'd closed my eyes, the flash of light was

bright enough to blind me for a second. I rubbed my eyes and when I could see again, Beth was smiling.

'What?' I asked. 'What can you see that's making you so happy?'

'That,' she said, pointing to the sign on the wall next to us. 'Castle Street. Isn't that where your dad lived when he was a little kid?'

'You're right,' I said. 'I'm so glad we don't have to go on a crazy, scary walk. This time Rico's landed us exactly where we need to be.'

'Good old Rico!' said Beth.

'Let's hope he's landed us *when* we need to be,' I said. 'It so won't be helpful if it's only last week – or tomorrow or something.'

'How are we going to figure it out?' said Beth. 'The houses are just normal houses, and there's no one around to ask.'

'Let's just wait and see,' I said. 'I'm sure we'll figure it out – eventually – and then we can go looking for my dad.'

Chapter Six

For a few minutes neither of us said anything. It's very strange not having any clue what day or month or year it is. After a bit, a huge purple car drove by.

'Look, Molly,' said Beth. 'A purple car – that has to be the weirdest—'

'Weirder than that?' I said as an orange car came from the opposite direction, followed by two yellow ones.

Beth laughed. 'This is like being in the 1980s again,' she said. 'What is it with the people in the past? Why are all the colours so bright? Haven't they heard of black or white or grey?'

'I guess not,' I said. 'Look over there.'

Just up the road, a group of teenagers came out of a house. Beth and I watched in silence as they walked

past us. All the girls and a couple of the boys had long, straight hair, parted in the middle. Their clothes were all crazy bright colours. One girl was wearing a huge, long-sleeved pink and green maxi-dress that looked a bit like a tent. The others were wearing trousers with the biggest flares I had ever seen. At first I thought that everyone was weirdly tall, before I noticed that they were all wearing shoes with huge, high platform heels.

I wanted to ask one of them what date it was, but I was afraid I'd burst out laughing before I could get the words out. Anyway, they didn't seem to notice Beth and me in our ordinary clothes – it was like we just faded into the background.

'Wow!' said Beth when the teenagers had disappeared around a corner. 'Did you see that boy's red shirt? I think it was made of silk.'

I giggled. 'And it had to have had the biggest collar in the history of the world – if there was a sudden gust of wind he might end up flying away.'

'And I know I sound like my dad, but those shoes they were wearing – if they fell off them I bet they'd break their legs.'

I thought about all the weird and wonderful clothes Beth and I had seen in the 1960s and 1980s. Maybe the people who looked the strangest were the coolest of all? Maybe one day I'll have kids who will laugh at the clothes I think are so great right now. I'm not looking forward to that.

'You're right, and ...' I stopped talking as a little boy who looked like he was about eight or nine came along the road. He was wearing check, flared trousers and a striped tank top over a yellow shirt. I wondered who picked out his clothes – and if they'd had their eyes tested lately.

'Let's ask this kid what date it is,' I said.

By now the boy was next to us. He stopped and stared at Beth and me.

'You look funny,' he said.

'So do—' Beth stopped when I pinched her arm.

There was no one else around and we needed to find out when we were.

I smiled at the boy, but he didn't smile back.

'Hi,' I said. 'Do you know what date it is?'

'No,' he said. 'And I don't care either.'

'Oh,' I said. 'Never mind. Do you know what year it is?'

He picked his nose and stared at me for a minute. 'I'm not stupid,' he said. 'Of course I know what year it is.'

'So would you mind telling us?' said Beth.

The boy said nothing as he examined whatever he'd picked out of his nose.

'Please,' said Beth. 'Can you tell us what year it is – before you have to head off to your fancy dress party?'

Luckily the boy didn't get her joke. 'It's 1975,' he said. 'And if you didn't know that, you must be a right pair of wallies.'

'1975,' I whispered to Beth as I quickly did the maths in my head. 'That means Dad's seven years old.'

'How could your dad be seven years old?' laughed the boy, who had somehow managed to hear me. 'You thought I was stupid, but you are the stupid ones. Stupid. Stupid. Stupid. Stupid. Stupid.'

He did a little dance as he sang the last words. I don't believe in hitting little kids, but if I did, that boy would have been in a lot of trouble. He was the most annoying creature I'd ever come across.

'Hey, kid,' said Beth suddenly. 'Do you know a boy called Eddie? He lives on this street.'

Now the boy laughed even more. 'You mean Eddie the Egghead? He lives in number seven – with his brother, Stephen the Swot – except now he's Sick Stephen the Swot.'

I had no clue what he was going on about. I really felt like thumping the kid, but Beth was calmer than me. I guess it wasn't her dad and uncle who were being insulted.

'Why do you call them those names?' she asked.

'Because they *are* a swot and an egghead,' said the

boy. 'They think they're so great, hanging around in their fancy treehouse with their crippled cat, writing their precious stories.'

I took a step towards him, but Beth pulled me back.

'What's your name?' she asked.

'Billy,' said the boy.

'Well, Billy,' said Beth, pulling her phone from her pocket, and pressing a few buttons. 'We don't like it when you call people names.'

'So what are you going to do about it?' he asked.

Beth was staring at him fiercely, but this kid didn't seem to scare easily.

'Oh,' said Beth. 'If we hear you saying stuff like that again, we might ask our pet to come out from the bushes over there where he's hiding. We'll tell him we don't like you – and if we don't like you, he *definitely* won't like you.'

'I'm so scared,' said Billy, grinning, and looking over towards the bushes. 'Is it a pet rabbit or a little fluffy kitten?'

Beth smiled a sweet smile, as she slipped her phone into her pocket. I smiled too when I saw that she was holding her thumb carefully over the screen.

'No,' she said. 'Our pet isn't a rabbit or a kitten. His name is Leo. Say hello to the little boy, Leo.'

Suddenly there was the loud sound of a lion roaring. I could tell that it was coming from Beth's pocket, but Billy was watching the bushes. The wind blew then, and the bushes rustled. Billy gave a little squeak of fear, and backed away.

'Tell me, Leo, do you like little boys who call names?' asked Beth.

There was another roar – even louder than the one before.

'I don't like him,' wailed Billy. 'Take him away.'

'We might,' said Beth. 'If you're good.'

'And if you point us towards Eddie's house,' I added.

'Eddie the......' began Billy, but he stopped talking when Beth took a small step towards him. 'Eddie

lives over there,' he said. 'In the house with the yellow door.'

'Thank you,' said Beth. 'See you around. Not!'

Billy started to walk quickly away from us. When he was far enough away, he turned back and shouted. 'You two girls are crackers,' he said. 'And so is your stupid pet.' Then he ran into a house and slammed the door behind him.

'What a horrible kid,' I said. 'Poor Dad and Stephen – imagine having to live near that little monster.'

'Nightmare,' said Beth. 'Anyway, we don't have time to worry about the neighbours. Let's go see what's happening in your dad's place.'

Chapter Seven

*W*e stood for a second outside number 7 Castle Street. When we went back to the 1960s and the 1980s we spent most of our time with Beth's mum, and with her uncle Graham. Now we were going to see my family, and that felt a bit weird.

'My grandparents live here,' I said. 'Are we supposed to just go up and ring the bell – and if we do, and someone answers, what are we going to say?'

'Well at least your grandparents won't recognize you,' said Beth. 'Didn't they both die when you were a baby? That means they've never before seen the wonderful thirteen-year-old you.'

'They've never seen the cute baby me either,' I said. 'It's 1975, remember? I'm not going to be born for years and years.'

'You're right – this time-travel stuff can be very

confusing. I can never—'

'Shhhh,' I said. 'Did you hear that?'

'What?'

'Be quiet and you'll hear it.'

We listened for a second, and then I heard it again. It was a little boy's voice, coming from the back garden of number 7.

'Come on, Pablo. You can do it.'

'That must be your dad,' whispered Beth.

'Or Stephen,' I said.

'It doesn't matter which,' said Beth. 'Let's go before he disappears.'

I thought about arguing, but Beth was already gone. I followed her as she ran through the front gate, up the path, and down along the side of the house.

The back garden was huge, with lawns as big as a football pitch, and giant flower beds filled with bright red and yellow flowers.

'I can't see anyone,' said Beth.

I was kind of glad about that. I wasn't sure I wanted

to see anyone, especially not the grandparents I couldn't remember. Mum had made them sound very scary – not the kind of people who'd welcome a time-travelling granddaughter wandering around their garden.

Then I looked along the path that ran towards the end of the garden, and saw something through the trees.

'Look,' I whispered. 'Look over there.'

'The treehouse,' whispered Beth. 'Come on, Moll, that's where he has to be.'

The two of us walked along the path until we came to a thick green hedge, way taller than us. There was an iron gate, which I opened, jumping when it squeaked loudly.

We were in a dark, wooded area that you could just barely see from the house. The grass was thick and long, and there were lots of pale pink and white wildflowers. There was a warm, damp smell that reminded me of summer and adventures.

'A secret garden!' said Beth. 'This is so cool. If I lived here I don't think I'd ever go indoors.'

We followed a grassy path towards the huge tree where the treehouse was, and stood for a second at the bottom of the ladder. All we could hear was the wind in the leaves, and a bird singing somewhere far away.

Before we could decide what to do next, a crooked door in the treehouse opened, and a little boy was looking down at us. He was wearing a light brown jacket with huge red pockets, and a collar that reached right out to his shoulders.

I stared at him for a minute. He had lots of hair (which I wasn't used to) and chubby cheeks, and a big gap where his front teeth should be – but his eyes were exactly the same.

'Dad?' I whispered.

'Eddie,' said Beth, louder. 'You *are* Eddie, aren't you?'

'Who are you?' he said. 'How do you know my

name? Mammy says I'm not allowed to talk to strangers.'

'I'm Molly,' I said. 'And my friend is called Beth.'

'And we're not strangers,' said Beth. 'We're ...'

'... family,' I said.

He looked at us suspiciously. 'You're not my family.' he said. 'I don't even know you. You're trying to trick me.'

He stepped back and started to close the door.

'Well, you see, sometimes families can be very big,' I said quickly. 'And you don't get to know everyone at the same time.' It felt weird to be speaking to my dad like he was a little kid. I was used to him explaining stuff to me.

He still didn't look convinced, and I could see he was a little bit scared. Part of me wanted to run up the ladder and give him a big hug – except I guessed that would freak him out completely.

I smiled at him. 'I promise you, Eddie,' I said. 'In the future you and I are going to get to know each

other very well.'

Beth put one foot on the ladder. 'This is a very cool treehouse,' she said. 'Could we come up and see what it's like inside?'

Eddie thought for a minute. 'I've got a cat,' he said.

I didn't know if that meant yes or no, but Beth started climbing up the ladder, and I followed close behind her.

Eddie moved backwards so we could get in through the tiny door and when we were inside, he closed it behind us.

The treehouse was fairly big, with plenty of room for the three of us to sit down and stretch our legs out in front of us. Over the door there was a shelf with some books and toy cars and a torch. In one corner was a big wooden box, like an ancient pirate's chest. On the lid there was a label – TOP SECRET. In another corner we could see a cat asleep on a fluffy red cushion.

'Pablo!' I said.

Eddie nodded. 'How do you know his name?'

'Oh, we've heard a lot about him,' said Beth. 'I bet he's only got three legs.'

'He's better than any cat with four legs,' said Eddie fiercely. 'When I found him in the garden, he could already run and jump and climb. He's the cleverest cat in the whole world.'

'He looks like he loves that fluffy cushion,' I said.

'We're getting him his own special bed,' said Eddie. 'Mammy's saving up Green Shield Stamps, and we only need one more book to have enough.'

'What are Green Shield...?' I started to ask, but then Pablo opened his eyes and sat up. Even though his front leg was missing, he was easily able to climb over Beth and me to get to Eddie. He sat on Eddie's knee and licked his face. Then he patted his cheek three times with his front paw.

Eddie smiled. 'I taught him to do that,' he said. 'And he doesn't do it to anyone else – only me.'

'He's adorable,' said Beth and I together.

'Pablo is my best friend in the whole world,' said Eddie, which was kind of cute and very sad.

Pablo curled up in Eddie's arms, and Eddie sang to him.

'This is his favourite song,' he said. 'I sing it to him every day.'

I didn't know that cats could have favourite songs, but Pablo certainly seemed to like this one. He purred loudly, then closed his beautiful green eyes, and fell fast asleep.

'Haven't you got a brother?' asked Beth.

'He's called Stephen,' said Eddie. 'I'm seven and he's eight.'

'Where is he today?' I asked. 'Why isn't he out here having fun with you and Pablo?'

'Stephen is sick,' said Eddie. 'He's in hospital.'

'Oh dear,' said Beth. 'Has he been there for long?'

Eddie shrugged. 'I can't remember - ages and ages and ages, I think.'

Little kids don't really understand time, so I won-

dered if Stephen had been sick for days or weeks or months.'

'But I guess you go and visit your brother every day?' I said. 'So you can tell him all about what you and Pablo are up to.'

Eddie shook his head. 'I asked, but Mammy and Daddy won't let me go. They say the hospital is only for sick kids.'

'That's harsh,' said Beth.

I made a face at her. Those were my grandparents she was dissing – and maybe it wasn't even their fault. Maybe hospitals had rules about child visitors in 1975.

'Mammy and Daddy go to the hospital every single day,' said Eddie. 'And they stay there for a long time. They don't play with me anymore. When Mammy puts me to bed she doesn't read me stories – she says she's too tired. Last night I cried for a story, so she started one, but she fell asleep after the first page.'

I could feel tears coming to my eyes. Eddie was

just a little kid, and couldn't really understand what was going on. None of this was his fault, but he was still having a hard time.

'Stephen must miss you and Pablo,' I said.

'Pablo is mine,' said Eddie. 'I'm the one who found him and minded him when he was a tiny baby kitten. Pablo is mine – only mine!'

'Sharing is caring,' I said, sounding a lot like my mum.

'I can share,' said Eddie. 'Sometimes I let Stephen play with Pablo and feed him and things like that. But Pablo will always love me the best.'

'OK,' I said. 'We get it. Pablo is yours.'

'Only mine,' he repeated.

Then I remembered I had a job to do. 'Before Stephen got sick I guess you two played out here a lot?' I said.

Eddie smiled a very cute, gap-toothed smile. 'Every single day,' he said. 'It's our favourite place in the universe.'

'What did you do?' asked Beth.

Now Eddie looked shy and embarrassed. 'If I tell you you'll laugh at me.'

'We won't, we promise,' I said.'

'We just do stupid things,' said Eddie, with his head down.

'Why don't you tell us and we'll decide if they're stupid or not,' I said.

He looked up again, and his innocent, hopeful face made me want to cry. Why was he so shy and lacking in confidence?

'Stephen and me wrote stories,' he said. 'We're going to be famous writers when we grow up – like Enid Blyton – so we have to practise a lot now. We write every day – well, we *did* write every single day, until Stephen got sick.'

'But writing's not stupid,' said Beth.

'Writing's really great!' I said. 'Don't give up, Eddie. I'd love if you grew up to be an author.'

As I said the words, I felt sad. That's the trouble

with time-travelling – you know how things are going to turn out. My dad's not a writer – well, not yet anyway – and neither is Stephen.

'Billy says writing's stupid,' said Eddie then. 'Billy says only sissies write stories. He calls Stephen and me bad names.'

'You shouldn't listen to Billy,' I said. 'I bet he's just jealous. He has no clue how good you are.'

'Stephen and me showed Billy one of our stories,' said Eddie. 'We wanted to show him that they weren't stupid.'

The look on his face told me that hadn't been a great idea. I wasn't sure I wanted to hear what happened next, but Eddie told us anyway.

'Billy grabbed the page and ran away,' he said. 'Then he read the story out loud to all the other kids. He put on a silly voice – and everyone laughed at us.'

To Beth and me, Billy was just a very annoying little boy, but I guess for a quiet seven-year-old like Eddie, he was totally scary.

'That's so mean,' I said. 'Did you tell your mum and dad what happened?'

'Yes,' his voice was quiet. 'Daddy said I need to learn to fight my own battles.'

'And what did your mum say?' I asked.

'She said, "Sticks and stones will break my bones but names will never hurt me".'

'That's not even true!' I said. 'Names can be really hurtful. We did this anti-bullying thing in school and it said name-calling can be very damaging.'

'So what happened next?' asked Beth.

'Now all the other kids call us names too,' said Eddie. 'Well they call me names. They can't call Stephen anything 'cause he's not here – and now no one will play with me.'

Eddie had tears in his eyes. Maybe his brother could have protected him from Billy the bully. Maybe the two of them could have been strong together, but on his own…? The poor little guy had no chance. I couldn't resist anymore. I leaned across Pablo, who

was still fast asleep, and hugged the kid who was going to grow up to be my dad.

'I'm too big for hugs,' he muttered as he pulled away from me.

'Billy's just a pathetic loser,' I said. 'All bullies are. You can still write stories – but maybe don't share them with Billy if he's not smart enough to appreciate them. Maybe keep them to yourself for a little bit.'

'I'm not going to write anymore,' said Eddie.

'But you said you love writing,' said Beth. 'You have to keep it up. You can't let Billy win.'

'Writing's stupid,' said Eddie.

'You don't really believe that?' I said.

'I think I do,' he whispered.

He looked up at me with his huge green-brown eyes, and I had to sit on my hands to stop myself from hugging him again.

'Eddie! Time for dinner. Come in quickly before it goes cold.'

The voice was coming from the back of the house.

'It's Mammy,' said Eddie, looking nervous. 'I've got to go.'

He put Pablo onto his cushion, and stroked his head.

'Er, Eddie,' I said. 'Maybe it's best if you don't tell your mum about ...'

He folded his arms and suddenly he looked older than seven.

'No one else is allowed up here 'cept Stephen and me. I'll be in trouble if Mammy knows you're here.'

'No need to mention it then,' said Beth.

'So will you come out here again later?' I asked, suddenly wanting to spend more time with the sweet little boy.

He shook his head. 'I have to help Daddy with jobs after dinner.'

'What kind of jobs?' I asked, looking at the skinny kid in front of me.

'Oh, you know,' he said. 'Boys' jobs – polishing all

the shoes in the house and emptying the bins.'

Beth giggled. 'And what would girls' jobs be?' she asked.

Eddie counted them off on his fingers. 'Mammy says cooking and washing-up and ironing are jobs for girls because girls aren't as strong as boys.'

I thought of my mum – she would kill anyone who talked like that. I smiled at Eddie. 'You're only a kid now,' I said. 'But one day you're going to grow up and get married – and, here's a little tip – maybe your life will be easier if you forget old-fashioned ideas like that.'

'Eddie! Come inside at once!' Now his mum sounded really angry.

'Coming, Mammy,' he called. 'Bye, Molly. Bye, Beth.'

And then my little-kid dad scrambled down the ladder and was gone.

Chapter Eight

'OMG!' said Beth. 'I think he must be the cutest little kid I've ever seen. Why do boys have to grow up?'

'Well, if that particular little boy hadn't grown up, I'd never have been born, and you and I wouldn't be having this conversation right now.'

'I guess. Hey, Moll, it was really nice seeing your adorable dad today, but it didn't really get us anywhere, did it?'

'You're right. Dad didn't sound like he was fighting with Stephen – he was just sad that he wasn't around – and I guess he felt a bit left out while his parents were fussing around Stephen, but would that be enough to make them grow up the way they did?'

'And Pablo is alive and well too. I'm glad about that because he's so sweet – but it doesn't help us under-

stand why your dad won't get a cat now that he's all grown up.'

'Maybe we got here a few years too early?'

Beth shook her head. 'I don't think so. Every time we've gone through Rico's door we've ended up where we need to be, so maybe …'

I jumped up. 'Maybe we need to get out of here. My scary granny could be along any minute, giving us "girls' jobs" to do.'

'OK,' said Beth, getting up too. 'Let's go for a walk. We might meet Billy again, and we can give him a hard time for picking on your dad. Maybe that would help things a bit.'

'I so don't fancy running through the back garden,' I said, as we climbed down the ladder. 'What if some-one sees us?'

'How fast can you run?'

'Not as fast as you.'

'Look,' she said then, pointing at a small hole in the hedge. 'I think we could get through there.'

So we went to where the hole was, made it a bit bigger, and wriggled through into a narrow laneway.

'Perfect,' said Beth, as we walked along the lane and ended up in front of Eddie's house. 'Our own secret entrance. Now, which way will we go?'

Just then two girls on a very funny-looking bike stopped beside us. It was bright purple, with red and yellow writing. It had high handlebars, a big back wheel and a small front wheel. The two girls were sitting, one in front of the other, on a long, black saddle. I know it's rude to stare, but I couldn't help it – it was the weirdest bike I had ever, ever seen.

One of the girls was staring back at me. 'What's the matter with you? Haven't you ever seen a Chopper before?'

'You mean a helicopter?' I said.

The girl rolled her eyes and slapped the bike's high handlebars. 'What swamp did you just crawl out of? *This* is a Chopper.'

'Oh,' I said. 'It's very nice. I've always wanted one

of those.'

'Thanks,' said the girl, suddenly all friendly. 'Do you two want to hang around with us?'

Before I could decide what to say, Beth decided for both of us. 'Sure,' she said. 'Let's all hang … around.'

'We can go to my place,' said the other girl. 'No one's home.'

Beth and I followed as the girls wobble-cycled a little way up the road, and into the front garden of a house. They dropped the bike against a hedge and for the first time I could see that each girl had a tartan scarf tied around her wrist. I wanted to ask why, but I was worried that they already thought Beth and I were idiots, so I kept my mouth shut.

'I'm Donna,' said one girl as she unlocked the front door.

'And I'm Pam,' said the other girl.

'We're Molly and Beth,' I said, as we followed them up the stairs and into a small bedroom.

'This is my room,' said Donna. 'Mum and Dad let

me decorate it myself. What do you think?'

I thought that it made my head hurt, but it didn't seem polite to say that. I looked around for a minute, trying to think of something nice to say. Next to me, Beth was silent too. Two of the bedroom walls were painted dark navy, and decorated with hundreds of stars that looked like they'd been cut out of tinfoil. A third wall was painted a sickly mauve colour, and had dark purple footprints going all the way up to the ceiling. The fourth wall was covered with posters of what looked like a boyband – a very weird boyband.

'Don't you just love The Bay City Rollers?' asked Pam.

'Er, sure we do,' said Beth.

'Totally,' I said, suddenly understanding why Pam and Donna had those weird scarves tied around their wrists.

What's not to love about five guys dressed in short baggy trousers, with tartan shirts and tartan scarves and stripy socks?

What's not to love about five guys with very dodgy haircuts who seem to need braces to hold up their pants?

'Wanna hear my favourite song of theirs?' asked Donna.

'That'd be great,' I said. Surely these guys couldn't sound as bad as they looked?

'Can you pass me that cassette, please?' asked Donna.

I had no clue what a cassette was, but she seemed to be pointing at a grey plastic thing on the dresser. I handed it to her and she put it into a big clunky machine. She pressed lots of buttons and I could hear weird squeaky noises, like someone was scraping their fingers up and down a blackboard. In the end she pressed another button, and the music started to play. Donna didn't seem to mind that it was already halfway through the song – she and Pam got up and danced around the room, waving their tartan scarves in the air, singing 'Bye, bye, baby' at

the top of their voices.

As the song came to an end, I could hear a slam-ming door and then a man's voice. 'For pity's sake, Donna, turn off that infernal racket – it's not even proper music – it's just noise.'

Beth and I jumped up. 'Molly and I had better go,' she said. 'Sounds like your dad is home.'

Her words didn't sound funny to me, but Donna and Pam fell around laughing. It was hard not to feel a bit insulted, and maybe Pam noticed that Beth and I didn't look too happy.

'Her dad's not here now,' she said.

'But I just heard him!'

She explained patiently, and when she was finished Beth and I stared at each other. 'So you're saying that when you hear a song you like, you run over and hold that giant-sized machine next to the radio and press those buttons, and it records the song, and anything else that's going on in the background too?' I said.

Donna nodded. 'I don't understand how you two

don't know that, but yeah.'

She pressed some more buttons on the machine. 'Milly ruined "Shang a Lang" when I taped it last week,' she said. 'Listen to this.'

Another jangly pop song started to play, and halfway through, I could hear loud howling and barking.

'Please say that Milly's a dog,' said Beth and everyone laughed.

After that, things were really nice. Donna and Pam might have had weird hairstyles and clothes and very strange taste in music, but in all the important ways, they were pretty much like Beth and me. Pam was worried about a history test that was coming up, and Donna was hoping to get picked for the basketball team.

Donna picked up a pair of jeans. 'I've just finished sewing these,' she said. 'Aren't they great?'

'You can sew?' I said.

'Sure I can,' said Donna. 'Can't you?'

'My granny showed me how to sew in a button

once,' I said. 'But that was ages ago, and I've forgotten how to do it.'

Donna held up the jeans so we could see them properly. They looked like they'd been pretty ordinary once upon a time, but Donna had cut one of the seams right up to the knee, and sewn a huge triangle of bright flowery material into the gap.

'They're lovely,' I said, wondering why anyone would turn sort-of-OK straight jeans into very weird, colourful flares. I guess fashion makes people do crazy things.

'Donna and I sew all the time,' said Pam. 'When your jeans get too short, you can sew some of the same material on to the ends – or you could use this,' she said, pointing to the hem of her own jeans. Now that I looked closely, I could see that her jeans really were much too short for her, but it wasn't obvious, because she had a strip of gold-coloured braid sewn to the ends – a good idea, except the braid looked a lot like the trimming on my granny's

favourite armchair.

'Where are your mum and dad, Donna?' asked Beth then.

'They're both at work,' she said. 'And, boy, am I glad about that.'

'I'd hate if my mum went out to work,' said Pam. 'I like having her home, baking cakes and making things nice for me when I get home from school.'

Donna rolled her eyes. 'It's 1975, you know, Pam. Women weren't put on earth to bake cakes and do housework.'

'It's not just housework,' said Pam. 'Who's supposed to mind the children if all the women go out to work?'

'And that's how women are meant to spend their lives?' said Donna.

'They wouldn't have to work every single minute,' said Pam. 'When the kids are at school, the mums can go to coffee mornings and things. That's what women do.'

I could hardly believe what I was hearing.

Could these girls not imagine a world where women could *choose* how to live their own lives?

And is there anything more embarrassing than being caught up in someone else's argument?

Then Pam smiled at Beth and me. 'Sorry,' she said. 'Donna and I have been having this fight nearly every day for the past two years.'

'What happened two years ago?' I asked.

'They changed the law – and Mum was able to go back to work.'

'There was a law against work?' said Beth.

Donna and Pam stared at her. 'Everyone knows that,' said Pam.

'How come you don't know that, Beth?' I asked her, giggling.

She gave me her evil look. 'You know I don't read the papers much, Molly,' she said in a fake-sweet voice. 'Why don't you explain the law to me?'

'Er, I'm not very good at explaining things,' I said.

'Will you tell her, Donna?'

Donna sighed. 'Anyone ever tell you two that you're a bit cracked?' she said.

But then she went on to explain. 'Mum used to work in the bank, and she really loved it, but, like all women, when she got married she had to give up her job.'

'She had to give up?' I said.

'Yeah,' said Donna. 'That was the law – and Mum hated not going out to work – but luckily they changed the law a couple of years ago – or Mum would still be hanging around all the time, annoying me.'

I tried to imagine a world where women had to choose between having a job and getting married – but I couldn't. It was much too scary for me.

'I'm glad women are getting so many rights these days,' said Donna.

'Like what?' I asked, not sure that I wanted to hear the answer.

'Oh,' said Pam. 'I don't think it's a good idea, but I heard that by the end of this year, women will be allowed to read the news on the television.'

At first I thought she was joking, but she looked perfectly serious. 'You mean—?'

Before I could finish my question, Donna pulled a magazine from under her pillow. 'Have you read this week's *Jackie* yet?' she asked.

Beth and I shook our heads so the four of us lay on the brightly patterned carpet and read. Four people reading one magazine is kind of dodgy anyway, but I wanted to see what kids in 1975 were into.

The first page had a big ad. 'PET ROCKS RULE', it said, with a picture of a stone on a pile of straw inside a cardboard box.

'What on earth are pet rocks?' I asked.

'They're just rocks,' said Pam. 'I can't believe you haven't heard of them. Everyone wanted one for Christmas last year.'

'But they are pets too,' said Donna. 'They come

with a manual, so you can teach them tricks.'

'What kind of tricks can a rock do?' I asked.

'Well the best one is playing dead,' said Donna, laughing. 'Pet rocks are really good at that.'

Now we all laughed, and Pam turned to the next page.

The magazine had lots of pictures of pop bands, all dressed in weird and wonderful clothes. There were heaps of stories about things to say to get boys to notice you, and things to wear to get boys to notice you. It was actually kind of boring.

For a minute Pam and Donna had a row about who was nicer – David Cassidy or David Essex. I had to admit that they both looked kind of cute – but a proper haircut would have made them a whole lot cuter.

Then Pam turned to a page that was a big ad for face cream. It told the story of a girl who had spots, but then used the cream every day, until her spots disappeared. In the end she was all excited, telling

her friends – 'I'm getting married – and it's all thanks to the super cream.'

'That's so lame!' said Beth.

'What do you mean?' asked Pam.

'That story,' said Beth. 'It's basically like, if you've got spots no one will marry you.'

'And if you get rid of your spots, your reward will be a lovely husband,' I said, giggling.

'Appearance shouldn't matter,' said Beth.

'But it *does* matter,' said Donna. 'Everyone knows that.'

'OK,' said Beth. 'I guess we all like to look our best, but it's not the most important thing in the world – and neither is getting a husband.'

'Isn't it?' said Pam, and I couldn't work out if she was joking or not.

'So what should the ad say?' said Donna.

I thought for a minute. 'I guess they need to sell their cream, so maybe they have to say that getting rid of your spots will change your life – even if that's

104

a big lie.'

'Molly's right,' said Beth. 'If you were sad before, I guess you'd still be sad afterwards – except without a spotty face.'

'But maybe the ad should say that when the girl's spots were gone, she got a great job in a tech company, or became an influencer or something?' I said.

'What's a tech company?' asked Donna. 'And an influencer?'

Pam was staring at Beth and me. 'You two girls are very ...'

I could guess what was coming next. I was enjoying hanging out with Donna and Pam, and for a minute I'd managed to forget how much the world had changed since 1975.

'Er, I think maybe it's time for us to go, Beth,' I said, getting up. 'It's been really nice, though. Thanks for letting us hang ou— I mean, hang around with you.'

'Let's meet up again soon,' said Donna. 'But not

this afternoon, because Mam and Dad are getting off work early, and we're all going to stay with my granny for the night.'

'Maybe we could meet tomorrow or the day after,' said Pam. 'Donna and I are planning to make a Swingball set. You can do it with us if you like.'

'You're going to *make* Swingball?' said Beth.

'Sure,' said Donna. 'All we'll need is a brush handle and a wire hanger, and a few other bits and pieces.'

'We made our own Monopoly game last week,' said Pam.

I smiled; that actually sounded like fun. Maybe my mum is right when she says that if we didn't spend so much time on our phones we'd have more time to be creative.

'We'd love to see you again, wouldn't we, Beth?' I said. 'But we live kind of far away, and we're not around here very much.'

Donna tore a piece off the cover of her *Jackie* magazine and wrote down her phone number. 'Here,' she

said. 'Ring me the next time you're around.'

'Or we could send you a—' I stopped and Donna finished my sentence, '—a letter? A postcard?' she said, looking confused.

'Forget it,' I said, smiling. 'If we're ever back here we'll give you a call.'

Beth got up. 'Oh,' she said. 'Before we go – do you happen to know Eddie and Stephen who live up the road?'

'Sure we do,' said Pam. 'My mum is friends with their mum. They're really cute little kids. It's a shame Stephen's been so sick, though.'

'Yeah,' I said. 'Has he been in hospital for long?'

'A good while,' said Donna.

'Nearly three months,' said Pam. 'I heard my parents talking about it yesterday – but he's coming home some time this afternoon.'

'That's brilliant news,' I said, so glad that my kid-dad wouldn't have to deal with Billy on his own anymore. 'That will be such a big surprise for Eddie.'

'But it's a shame about the cat, though,' said Pam.

'I know Pablo only has three legs,' I said. 'But that really isn't a problem. He can—'

'That's not what I mean,' said Pam.

'Then what do you mean?' I asked.

'My mum says that when Stephen comes home he will be very weak. He won't be able to play outside for ages and he will have to stay away from germs. Stephen's parents think that cats carry germs so ...'

'So?' said Beth and I together.

'So they have to get rid of the cat,' said Pam.

'When you say "get rid of"?' said Beth.

'They're sending him to the animals' home,' said Pam. 'Eddie's dad is going to take him after they bring Stephen home from hospital. They haven't told Eddie yet.'

'But that's not fair!' I said. 'Taking that cat totally sucks, but if they do it without warning, Eddie won't even have any time to get used to the idea. He loves that cat so much – it'll break his little heart.'

'The poor kid,' said Pam. 'But I suppose his parents know best. His dad said "a clean quick break" is the way to do it.'

'That's the cruellest thing I've ever heard,' I said. 'Come on, Beth, we've got to go over there and ...'

'And what?' asked Beth.

'I have no clue,' I said. 'But we've got to do something.'

Chapter Nine

*B*eth and I said goodbye to our new friends and raced across to Eddie's house.

Unfortunately, Billy was walking past. 'Are you waiting for Eddie the Egghead?' he said. 'He's a sissy – he loves playing with girls – ha, ha.'

That kid had a very bad memory. Had he already forgotten about our imaginary pet called Leo? Beth pulled her phone out of her pocket, but I shook my head. We didn't have time for this now.

'Go away, you annoying boy,' I said, and to my surprise, Billy ran away, looking a tiny bit scared.

Just then a big blue car pulled into Eddie's driveway. Beth and I ducked behind a bush and watched as a tall man in a dark suit got out. He opened the back door of the car, and picked up a blanket-wrapped bundle with two skinny legs dangling from it. As the

man turned around we could see Stephen's face. He was pale and very sick-looking – like he hadn't been out in the fresh air for months and months.

The front door opened and a woman wearing huge flares and a tie-dyed shirt came out.

'My precious boy,' she said, stroking Stephen's face. 'Home at last. I've made your favourite dinner – gammon steaks and Arctic roll for dessert.'

I had no clue what Arctic roll was, but dad once told me that the food he hated most in the world was gammon steaks.

'And wait till you see the new shelves I put up in your bedroom, Stephen,' said his dad. 'They'll be perfect for all your new toys.'

As they fussed around Stephen, Eddie appeared in the doorway.

'Say hello to your brother,' said Eddie's mum, as if they'd never met before.

'Hi, Stephen,' said Eddie.

'Hi, Eddie,' said Stephen in a quiet, weak voice.

'Pablo and I missed you,' said Eddie. 'We're glad you're home.'

Stephen smiled. 'I'm glad too,' he said. 'When I'm feeling better we can …'

Then his dad interrupted. 'Don't just stand there, Eddie,' he said. 'Carry Stephen's toys inside for him.'

So Eddie leaned in to the back of the car and picked up two huge bags of toys, and followed his parents and brother into the house.

I could feel tears come to my eyes. 'This is all so sad,' I whispered. 'The boys are trying their best, but their parents aren't helping at all. Can't they see how lost and left out Eddie feels? Can't they see that asking him to carry Stephen's toys is really mean?'

'I'd love to march right in there and tell those two grown-ups what a huge mistake they're making,' said Beth. 'But they don't seem like the kind of grown-ups who think kids' opinions matter.'

'You're right,' I said. 'If we say something, I know it wouldn't make any difference – or it might even

make things worse for poor Eddie. How can they be so cruel?'

'Poor Stephen looks really sick – and maybe his parents can't cope with that. Maybe they're so busy trying to make him better, they've pretty much forgotten their other son.'

Beth was better than me at seeing both sides of the story – or maybe I just couldn't get past the lost look on my little dad's face.

'But that's so ...'

'I guess times were different then – or now – or wherever we are,' she said. 'In our real lives, my dad's friend's son got very sick a few years ago, and all his brothers and sisters went to the hospital every week for family therapy. I didn't understand why at the time, but I totally get it now.'

'Oh, I'm glad we live when we do,' I said. 'This is all so sad – and soon ... Pablo. Oh, Beth, what are we going to do?'

Beth put her arms around me. 'I'm so sorry, Molly,'

she said. 'This is too big for us. No offence, but your grandparents look totally scary. We can say what we like, but I don't think there's anything we can do to save Pablo. If we march in there and try to rescue him, they'll probably call the police or something – and I so don't like the idea of going to jail in 1975.'

I started to cry. 'Maybe you're right,' I said. 'But there's no way I'm letting my dad, Eddie, face this on his own. I'm not moving, and if he needs me, I'll be right here.'

'*We'll* be here,' said Beth, and the two of us sat down on the footpath to wait.

* * *

A while later, the front door opened again, and my granddad came out, carrying a large cardboard box with holes cut in the side. He put the box on the ground and used a key to open the back door.

A second later Eddie appeared. His eyes were all

red and puffy.

'Daddy, you forgot Pablo's favourite toy mouse,' he said, holding up a gross, dirty-looking thing.

His dad lifted up a corner of the box and Eddie put the mouse inside. A little black nose appeared in the open corner. Eddie knelt down next to the box.

'Be a good boy, Pablo,' he said. 'Eat up all your dinner every day, so you won't get sick – and stay away from dogs – some of them can be really mean. I love you, Pablo. You're the best cat in the whole world. One day, when I'm big, I'll come and get you.'

His dad sealed up the box, put it on the back seat and slammed the door.

Tears were pouring down Eddie's little cheeks – almost as many as were pouring down mine. Beth held my hand tightly, as I did my best to cry quietly.

'Tell them he likes warm milk – and chicken,' said Eddie. 'Tell them that he's afraid of balloons. Tell them that he loves it when you tickle under his chin. Tell them ...'

His dad patted his shoulder. 'I know this isn't easy, son,' he said. 'But you have to be a big, brave boy – for Stephen's sake. I'm sure Pablo will find a very nice home, where they will love him as much as you do. Now why don't you go inside and play with your brother?' Eddie nodded. His dad stepped towards the car and then stopped. 'One more thing,' he said. 'You must never tell Stephen the truth about why Pablo has to go.'

'But—'

'Do you hear me? Never. Ever. That poor sick boy isn't strong enough to know things like that. We'll just tell him that Pablo was getting too hard for us to manage. That's the best thing for everyone.'

'That's so messed up,' I said

'Agreed,' said Beth. 'No wonder your dad doesn't like his brother. I know none of this is Stephen's fault, but I still kind of hate him right now.'

For a minute, Eddie stood in the driveway, watching as his dad drove away. I could hear his sobs as he

used the sleeve of his ugly stripy jumper to wipe his tears.

I took a step towards him, but Beth pulled me back.

'I just want to give him a hug,' I said.

'I know,' she said. 'But if his mum comes out and sees two weirdly-dressed randomers hugging him–'

Then Eddie started to run. He raced along the driveway and down the side of the house.

'The treehouse,' I whispered, as I jumped up and ran down the lane, with Beth following me.

By the time we'd crawled through the gap in the hedge, and climbed up the ladder, Eddie was already sitting in the treehouse, hugging Pablo's fluffy red cushion.

'Oh, Eddie,' I said, as I crawled over and hugged him. For a second he sat there stiffly, and it was like hugging a dummy from a shop window, but then he hugged me back, and cried until the front of my hoodie was all wet. Finally he pulled away from me.

'Pablo's ... gone,' he said, barely able to get the

words out between his sobs. 'Daddy took Pablo away and he never even got his new bed. Daddy said I'm not supposed to cry. He said it will make a man of me.'

That was so cruel. Eddie wasn't a man. He was only a very small, very sad little boy.

'We're so sorry,' I said. 'But we heard what your dad said – he thinks Pablo will find a lovely home.'

'He already *had* a lovely home,' said Eddie. 'Until Stephen came back. I *hate* Stephen.'

'I know you're sad and angry now,' I said. 'But it's not Stephen's fault is it? He can't help being sick, and maybe he feels—?'

'I don't care,' said Eddie. 'I hate, hate, *hate* him! I only love Pablo and I am *never* going to get another pet – ever, ever in my whole life.'

The poor little boy was crying again, and I had no idea what to do. I wished my mum was there to give me some advice. My dad actually was there, but he was only seven, and not a whole lot of help.

'Hey, Eddie,' said Beth. 'Maybe one day …'

Before she could finish, there was a loud shout. 'Eddie! Where on earth have you got to? Stephen is hungry and it's time for lunch – come inside at once.'

'It's Mammy,' said Eddie, like we didn't already know and fear that voice.

He put the red cushion carefully in the corner, and crawled towards the ladder.

'Will you girls be here later?' he asked.

Beth and I looked at each other.

'We're not sure,' said Beth gently. 'We might have to go … on a journey.'

'But we promise we'll see you again someday,' I said.

'Someday sounds like a long time,' said Eddie.

Then his mother called again, and he scrambled down the ladder and was gone.

* * *

'Oh, Molly,' said Beth, as we crawled through the hedge into the lane. 'I think we've figured out what happened to Pablo, and why things went so wrong between Eddie and Stephen, but I'm sorry we didn't manage to change anything – except now you're really sad too.'

'Thanks, Beth,' I said. 'I wish things could be different. I wish there was something we could do to help – but there isn't. We've just been wasting our time.'

Neither of us said anything as we walked down the lane and onto the road. We walked along until the houses disappeared, and all we could see were fields and trees. We walked for a long time. It was nice and peaceful, but I had no clue where we were going.

Were we supposed to just go back home?

'I guess we could—' I was saying, when things suddenly started to happen very quickly.

Beth stepped out onto the road without looking.

There was a big screech of brakes as a car tried to stop.

There was a weird crumpling sound as the front of the car hit Beth.

Then my best friend lay on the road with her eyes closed, and a tiny trickle of blood on her cheek.

Chapter Ten

'Beth!' I screamed as I ran and kneeled next to her. 'Talk to me. Are you OK? Please say you're OK. If anything happens to you—'

Beth's eyelids flickered, and I was never so happy to see her beautiful, pale blue eyes staring up at me.

Then she turned her head, and I could see a small puddle of blood on the road.

'Oh, Beth!' I said, as I held her hand and started to cry.

By now the driver of the car was standing next to us.

'I'm so sorry,' she said. 'Is she all right? She just stepped out in front of me. I tried to stop, but I couldn't – there wasn't enough time.'

Beth started to get up and blood trickled down the back of her neck. 'I'm fine,' she said. 'Absolutely fine.

Good as new actually.'

The woman took off her scarf and pressed it to the back of Beth's head.

'Hold still, dear,' she said. 'Until we see how bad this is.'

I used my sleeve to wipe the blood from Beth's cheek. It looked kind of scary on my white hoodie.

'I guess I got a few little scratches,' said Beth. 'But I'm practically fine.'

The woman made Beth sit on the footpath, and she sat down beside her. 'I'm sure you're fine,' she said. 'But I don't like the look of this cut on your head. I've done a first-aid course and I know it's better to be safe than sorry. Do you mind if I ask you a few questions, so we can be sure you're not concussed or anything?'

'Sure,' said Beth. 'I'm good at quizzes. I've got to level three hundred and sixty on my quiz app.'

The woman gave her a funny look. I guess quiz apps weren't a thing in 1975.

'So tell me, dear,' she said. 'Who is the president?'

'Easy peasy,' said Beth.

Beth's good at all kinds of random stuff, but I guessed she was forgetting one important detail. I wanted to kick her, and remind her that we were in 1975, but I was afraid of injuring her even more.

'Er, Beth ...' I said, but she interrupted me and said the president's name.

'Dear me,' said the woman. 'That's not right, but maybe you're too young to know the right answer.'

'Oh,' said Beth. 'For a second there I forgot we're back in the ... I mean ... I bet the president now is one of the Marys isn't it? They were around for ages and ages. Is it Mary McAleese or, what was the other one called, Molly?'

The woman laughed. 'I see your sense of humour is intact anyway. The thought of a woman president! It would be nice, but I don't see that happening any time soon.'

I smiled. When I was little I thought the president

had to be a woman.

'Tell me instead, dear, what day it is?' asked the woman.

'Er….' said Beth looking at me for inspiration. I shook my head. I knew that in the present it was Sunday, but that wasn't much help.

The woman was looking worried now. 'What month is it then?' she asked.

Beth looked confused again. 'I know it's 1975,' she said. 'Is that any good?'

The woman stood up. 'You're probably fine, but I can't take any chances, so I will have to drive you home. Do you live around here?'

'Er no,' I said. 'We live very far from here – and it's really hard to get to.'

'And where are your parents?' She looked up and down the street as if they were going to magically appear.

My dad wasn't too far away, but since he was only seven, he wasn't going to be much use.

'Are you sisters?' asked the woman then.

Beth and I looked at each other. I wondered if families like ours existed in 1975.

'We're friends,' I said.

'Best friends,' said Beth.

The woman twisted her hands. 'I wish there was a phone box nearby, so I could ring the police or an ambulance for you.'

Once again, I wondered how people actually managed to live in the olden days. What did they do in emergencies? Were they supposed to travel with a carrier pigeon in their cars in case they had an accident and weren't near a phone box?

'There's nothing for it,' said the woman then. 'I'll have to bring you to the hospital.'

She took Beth by the arm, stood her up and practically pushed her into the front seat of the car.

'I'm fine,' said Beth. 'Really. You can just go. Molly will take care of me, won't you?'

'I won't hear of it,' said the woman. 'You need to

be checked out by a doctor. That cut might need stitches.'

Beth was looking desperately at me through the open door of the car. I thought about grabbing her and running away over the hedge and through the woods. But she looked paler than I had ever seen her. What if she really was injured? We were far away from everyone we knew, and I didn't want to take any stupid chances.

'I think this lady's right, Beth,' I said. 'Let's go to the hospital – and then when they say you're OK, we can go ... home.'

'Good advice,' said the woman. 'And when we get to the hospital, you can telephone your families, and they can come and pick you up.'

So the woman got into the driver's seat, and I climbed over Beth and got into the back. I reached for the seat belt and then noticed there wasn't one – not even in the front! So I crossed my fingers and hoped that the woman was a good driver as we set off

for the hospital.

* * *

Luckily the hospital was really close – quite near Eddie's house on Castle Street. When we got there, the woman insisted on getting a wheelchair and wheeling Beth into the emergency room. As I watched, I couldn't make up my mind if it was very funny or very scary.

When we got inside, the woman handed me some funny-looking coins and pointed to a payphone.

'Please call your parents and Beth's parents and let them know what happened.'

I took the coins and went over to the payphone. I'd seen one when we were time-travelling before, and I was fairly sure I could remember how to work it, but that didn't really matter anyway.

Who was I supposed to call?

So I put the coins into the phone and pressed a few

random numbers, and then pretended to be waiting for someone to answer. After a minute or two I pressed another button and got the coins back. Then I did the same thing with a few more random numbers. When I got the coins back for a second time, I went back to where Beth and the woman were waiting.

'No one's home in my place or in Beth's,' I said, glad for once that mobile phones weren't invented yet. 'I guess our parents are shopping or working or something. I'll try again in a little while.'

'Oh, dear,' said the woman. 'I'd better talk to the staff and see what they've got to say.'

After that there was a big row, because the receptionist wasn't very happy about a woman landing in with two kids she didn't even know.

'Where are the parents or guardians?' she kept saying. 'I can't accept responsibility for unaccompanied children.'

So we sat and waited for another while and every

twenty minutes or so I went to the payphone and pretended to call our imaginary grown-up parents, and pretended to be surprised when no one answered.

After a while the woman stood up. 'I'm very sorry, but I need to leave,' she said. 'My mother is ill, and I have to bring her some medication and prepare her dinner.'

So she got two pieces of paper and wrote her name and address and phone number on each. She gave one to the receptionist and handed the other one to Beth.

'Please ask your parents to contact me,' she said. 'And tell them that I deeply regret what happened.'

Beth and I smiled at her. I felt sorry for the woman. She was nice, and it wasn't her fault that Beth had stepped right out in front of her car, was it?

Soon after the woman left, a nice nurse came over and sat next to us.

'It's strange that you haven't managed to contact your parents, Beth. Can you give me your phone

number, so the receptionist can try again?'

'Oh,' said Beth. 'I've actually forgotten my own phone number. How weird is that?'

'That might be the shock of the accident,' said the nurse. 'Can you tell me please, Molly?'

Didn't she know that the accident was just as shocking for me? Call me a wuss, but it's never a lot of fun seeing your best friend lying on the road, bleeding.

'Oh,' I said. 'Er, I think ... I mean ...'

I thought about making up a number, but I had no clue what a phone number in 1975 would even look like.

How many digits was it supposed to have?

What if I accidentally made up a real number, and someone answered and said they'd never heard of Beth?

Then Beth nudged me. 'I remember now,' she said. 'You have my number written down, don't you, Molly? I think you put it in your pocket.'

At last I remembered Donna's phone number. I smiled when I remembered that she and her parents were going away for the night. Hopefully they were already gone.

'Of course,' I said. 'Silly me.'

The nurse took Donna's phone number and put it into the pocket of her snowy white uniform. 'Don't you worry,' she said. 'We'll keep trying, but in the meantime, we have procedures for dealing with unaccompanied minors. We will take Beth to an examination room now, and see what's going on. Is that OK with you both?'

I could see tears coming to Beth's eyes, and I knew it was my turn to be brave.

I hugged her quickly. 'I know you're going to be fine,' I said. 'We're all just being super-careful. In half an hour we'll be on our way home, and we'll be laughing about all this.'

But I didn't feel very brave when they wheeled Beth away and I didn't feel very brave and I had to sit

on my own in the huge cold waiting room.

I felt even less brave an hour later when the nice nurse came back and said that they couldn't find anything seriously wrong, but because she had bumped her head, they were going to keep Beth in hospital overnight – as a precaution.

Now I started to cry. This was all getting much too scary. Beth had never been in hospital since she was born, and back then she had her mum with her to hug her and make her feel safe. Now she had to go through it without her dad or anyone to take care of her.

And if she stayed in hospital for the night, what on earth was I supposed to do?

The nurse put her arm around me. 'Now, now,' she said. 'I'm sure Beth is perfectly fine, and soon your mammy and daddy will be here and everything will be hunky-dory.'

That made me cry even more. Even if my kid mum and dad showed up, I'd have to wait years and years

for them to grow up enough to take care of me, and maybe I'd always be older than them anyway, and ...

I put my head down on the nurse's shoulder and cried like a little baby.

Chapter Eleven

a bit later, when my eyes were still all red and puffy, the nurse brought me to Beth's room. Beth was sitting up in bed, wearing an ugly blue nightie with PROPERTY OF REGIONAL HOSPITAL stamped all over it. In front of her was a huge plate of sandwiches and biscuits, a cup of milk and a bundle of *Jackie* magazines.

'I'll see if they've had any luck tracking down your parents,' said the nurse. 'And I'll let you two girls chat. I know what girls your age are like – full of little secrets.'

Beth and I smiled at the nurse as she backed out and closed the door behind her. She had no clue about the biggest secret of all.

The cut on Beth's cheek was tiny and had already stopped bleeding.

'What about the cut on your head?' I asked. 'Did you have to get stitches?'

She shook her head. 'They said scalp wounds bleed easily. They cut away a bit of my hair and put a plaster on the cut. Want to see?'

She held back her hair and I was happy to see a small little plaster that didn't look scary at all – and wouldn't even be easy to see under Beth's long hair.

I hugged her. 'I'm so sorry,' I said. 'This is all my fault. If I hadn't brought you back in time—

'Hey,' she said. 'It's not like you dragged me here, kicking and screaming. I wanted to come with you.'

'Yeah, but—'

'Look, Molly. You came with me when we found my mum, and when we were trying to help Graham. I'm really happy we tried to do something for your family for once. And anyway, this place isn't so bad. Everyone's been really nice to me.'

'Yeah,' I said. 'It's totally great – except you're stuck here for the night and I'm ...' I started to cry again.

'Hey,' said Beth. 'It's OK. You can sleep here on the floor next to me – or in the bed with me, if they'll let us. Now how about a sandwich? They're totally delicious.'

I suddenly remembered that I hadn't eaten for more than forty years. I ate some sandwiches, and drank loads of the milk, and after that I felt a small bit better.

I sat on the bed next to Beth and we read the magazines. The problem page was our favourite, and while some of the problems were a bit weird, others were kind of like the normal things that happen to Beth and me.

Much later the kind nurse came in again. 'I'm afraid it's time for you to go home, Molly,' she said. 'Visiting hours are long over, and our patient needs to get her beauty sleep.'

'I thought maybe I could wait until Beth's parents get here,' I said, like I didn't know that was never happening.

The nurse shook her head. 'That's out of the question,' she said. 'Children who aren't patients aren't allowed here after six. Do you live near here? Will you be able to walk home on your own?'

'Yes,' I said. 'I live on Castle Street.'

'That's perfect,' said the nurse. 'You'll be there in no time – and you can come back and see Beth first thing in the morning if you like. I expect her parents will be here long before that, but I'm sure they won't mind if you come along too.'

'But ...'

I didn't know what to say. If I told the nurse I had nowhere to go, she was going to start asking very awkward questions – the kind of questions that Beth and I couldn't possibly answer.

I've seen *Annie* the musical, five times and I so didn't want Beth and me to end up with someone like Miss Hannigan looking after us!

The nurse patted my head. 'Say goodnight to your friend,' she said. 'I'll be back in five minutes, and I

expect you to be gone by then.'

'Hey,' said Beth when the nurse was gone. 'Maybe you could hide here in the room, and then jump into bed with me when everything's quiet.'

It was a nice thought, but I could see it was crazy. The bed was up on high legs; anyone who came in would easily see me. Apart from that, the only furniture was a small locker that would have been a good hiding place – if I were a tiny baby.

'It's no good,' I said. 'I'll have to go.'

'But where? You can't walk around on your own for the night. It's too dangerous.'

'A 1970s sleepover would have been fun,' I said. 'It's a pity Donna's gone away for the night, and we have no clue where Pam even lives. The only other person we know around here is Eddie, but I can hardly—'

'That's it!' said Beth.

'What's it?'

'It's perfect. You can go to Eddie's place—'

'And knock on the door and tell my grandparents

that I'm Eddie's daughter, and can I stay the night, because my friend's in hospital and I'm too afraid to go through Rico's door on my own, and I'm sorry that Stephen is sick, but it was still really mean of them to give Pablo away like that?'

Beth giggled. 'That wasn't exactly my plan,' she said. 'I thought you could sneak into the treehouse, and spend the night there. I'd say it's cosy and warm, and—'

Suddenly I felt scared and angry at the same time. 'It's easy for you to talk about cosy and warm when you've got a bed to sleep in, and magazines to read, and a bell to ring for nice nurses to bring you food and drinks. I'll be on my own and scared and—'

'I'm sorry,' said Beth, leaning over and hugging me. 'How about if I sneak out and go with you?'

She was being so nice I couldn't feel angry anymore. 'No,' I said. 'We're not taking any stupid chances. The doctors said you need to be in hospital, so that's what's going to happen.'

'But you—'

'And besides, there's no way you can sneak out – there's a desk at the end of the corridor, with a line of nurses all ready to catch you and bring you back to bed.'

'I guess you're right,' said Beth. 'And they took away my clothes, so I might look a bit conspicuous running around in this weird nightie. Hey, Moll, we both know no parents will be coming to claim me any time soon, so can you bring me some clothes so I can escape tomorrow?'

'And where am I supposed to get clothes, except for the ones I'm wearing? I've only got the few coins that woman gave me – I'm no expert on 1975 money, but if it's just enough to make a phone call, I'm guessing it's not enough to buy you a fancy pair of flares and a shiny shirt, all accessorized with a tartan scarf for you to wear around your wrist.'

Beth laughed. 'You're a clever girl. See what you can do.'

I knew that if I had been the girl in the bed, Beth would have trekked the country to find me an escape outfit, so I nodded.

'Thanks,' she said. 'And hey, take these.'

She used a paper serviette to wrap up the last of the sandwiches and handed them to me. 'You can have a midnight feast,' she said.

A midnight feast on your own is no fun, but I knew she was trying to be nice.

'Thanks,' I said.

I could hear the squeak-squeak sound of the nurse's shoes coming along the corridor, and I didn't feel ready for more awkward questions, so I gave Beth a quick hug, and then I set off on my journey.

Chapter Twelve

It wasn't a long walk, but even so, it was almost completely dark by the time I got to Castle Street, which was quiet and a bit creepy. Inside Eddie's house, the lights were on, and I could see the family sitting around the table, eating. Eddie was leaning forward, and eating really fast, like someone was going to steal the plate away before he was finished. I had to smile – my dad still eats exactly the same way.

His mum said something to Eddie, and when he answered, I could see that he was laughing, and that made me feel good – maybe things weren't as bad as they had seemed that afternoon. Maybe little kids can forget – for a while.

I stood there for a long time, watching. When they had finished eating, his mum cleared the table, and the others just sat there – which seemed a bit mean

because I guessed she'd done all the cooking too.

When his mum came back into the room, everyone went to sit on the couch. His mum tucked a big blanket around Stephen's skinny legs. She didn't notice Eddie staring at her while she stroked Stephen's hair – but I did. I wondered if kids with brothers and sisters are jealous all the time.

How do mums and dads share out the hugs and the kisses so no one feels left out?

Maybe I'm lucky to be an only child.

Or maybe I'm really, really lucky to be an only child who lives in the same house as her very best friend.

My dad was just a kid, and I didn't really know the other people, but still I couldn't help feeling left out, like I should be in there with my family. After a bit, his mum got up and pulled the curtains closed. I know it was stupid, but I couldn't help feeling that she was deliberately shutting me out. It was the loneliest feeling in the world.

Luckily the moon gave enough light for me to find

my way down the lane and through the gap in the hedge. I climbed up the ladder, pushed open the door of the treehouse, and went inside.

When I'd been with Beth and Eddie, the treehouse seemed cool and fun, now it was dark and cold and scary. I'm not actually *scared* of the dark, but I don't like it very much either, and I really wished my phone wasn't dead. I shivered, wondering if it was too soon to curl up and cry. Then I remembered the torch I'd seen earlier. I felt around in the dark, and after I'd touched something sticky, and something that might have been a heap of dead flies, my fingers reached the cool hard plastic of the torch.

'Please have batteries,' I whispered as I felt for the switch. 'Please, please have batteries.'

As I slid the switch, the treehouse filled with a weak, yellowish light. 'Yesss!' I whispered. It's funny how little things can be so important at times like this.

With the light, I could examine the place more

closely. Behind the door I found real treasure – a thick woolly rug. I wrapped the rug around myself, propped the torch on the floor, and ate a sandwich to make myself feel better.

When I'd finished eating, I tracked the torch along the walls, looking at cobwebs and rusty nails. If Beth had been there, this could have been a wonderful adventure, but on my own ...

Then I saw the wooden box with the TOP SECRET label. I scooched over towards it and put my hand on the lid. For a tiny second I felt guilty, but then I got over it – after all, I was family, so the sign probably wasn't meant for me.

I lifted the lid slowly, not sure what I was hoping to see. A flask of hot soup would have been nice, or maybe a games console so the night would pass quickly.

For a second I was disappointed when I saw that the box was full of old exercise books.

'Yippee!' I thought. Lots of old homework belong-

ing to Eddie and Stephen. Maybe I could pass the time by seeing if they were any good at maths or geography back in the day? Lately, Dad has been giving me a hard time if I don't get top marks in every single test I do; maybe this was my chance to see exactly how great he was when *he* was at school. Maybe I'd get really lucky and find out that he was rubbish at something. But then I picked up the first book, and smiled.

The cover was decorated with drawings of monkeys and tigers. At the bottom, in wobbly capital letters I read – 'ADVENSHUR IN THE JUNGLE BY STEPHEN AND EDDIE'.

I'd found the stories that Eddie had told me about! There were loads and loads of them, and all of a sudden, I knew exactly how I was going to pass the hours until I was tired enough to go to sleep.

* * *

There were heaps of spelling mistakes, but 'Adven-shur in the Jungle' was a great story. Every now and then the handwriting changed, and I figured that was where one boy got tired of writing, and the other one took over. The hero of the story was a boy called Hector, who was afraid of everything, but still managed to do incredibly brave stuff, like rescuing babies from tigers, and swimming through crocodile-infested waters to deliver important messages to the queen. Some of the story was funny and some of it was sad, and all of it was really exciting.

When I was finished reading, I closed the book and put it on the rug next to me. I wondered if Eddie had any clue that one day he was going to grow up and leave his darling little girl behind and go and live in the jungle. Did he ever guess that he'd come back from the jungle years later, and be all mixed up and sad and lonely?

After the jungle story, I read one where Hector was on a pirate ship, and one where he went trekking to

the North Pole, and then five or six more.

I felt sad when I got to the last line of the last book. I felt like Hector was a real boy, and I wanted to know more about him. I wanted him to have more adventures. Eddie and Stephen were only little kids, but already they were great at writing. Dad sometimes wrote me letters when he was away, and they were always hilarious, but how come I'd never heard about these stories? How come Dad and Stephen hadn't gone on to be writers? They could have been like JK Rowling, and we'd all have been famous.

Had Billy the bully managed to ruin everything?

I carefully put the books back into the box and closed the lid. Then I noticed the corner of a page sticking out from under the box. I was excited as I pulled it out – maybe I could have one more Hector story before settling down to sleep.

But this wasn't a long exciting story about a boy adventurer, with different handwriting every few lines. This was just one page, with only one kind of

handwriting, and on the top it said – 'THE BOY WHO DISAPPEARED, BY ONLY EDDIE'.

I sat back and started to read.

Once upon a time there was a boy called Eddie who lived with his mammy and daddy and big brother Stephen and his cat called Pablo who only had three legs but was still brillyant. Everyone was happy cept on the days when Billy called them names and sometimes Eddie cried then and Stephen told him jokes until he wasn't sad anymore. Then Stephen went to hostipal and it was very bad. Stephen got lots of toys and Beano comics and fizzy drinks and a pet rock and an eevil kneevel stunt bike and Mammy and Daddy didn't love Eddie anymore but only Stephen the sick boy.

The end

By the time I came to the last lines, I was crying so

much I could barely read. That poor, poor little kid! Did he really believe his mum and dad didn't love him anymore?

And that story had to have been written before Eddie knew that Pablo had to go. How was he supposed to feel when Stephen came back home, and the price for that was losing his precious cat? He must have thought that the whole world was ganging up against him.

I sat up and wiped my eyes and tried to think straight. My mum was probably right when she said that Eddie's parents were good people, but how did good people manage to get things so wrong? They were worried about Stephen, but how come they couldn't see that their other little boy was so sad?

The light from the torch was getting dimmer, and I guessed that the batteries were running out. I didn't want it to go dead completely, so I switched it off and then curled up in my blanket, rested my head on Pablo's pillow, and fell asleep.

Chapter Thirteen

The sound of birds singing woke me up – I guess that's the downside of sleeping in a tree.

I had no clue what time it was, but it was just starting to get bright. I peeped out the door of the treehouse, but everything was quiet. I was stiff and hungry, and I really, really wanted to get to Beth so I could tell her about the Hector stories – and have a hug.

I folded up the blanket, and put Pablo's cushion back where I had found it. Then I opened up the box of stories. I picked up one story and looked at it for a long time. I felt like I had a lot of power in my hands and I wasn't sure how to use it. Would young Eddie be really sad that the story was gone? Or would old Eddie be really happy to see it again?

In the end, I folded the little book, and shoved it

into the pocket of my hoodie.

I climbed down the ladder and was heading for the gap in the hedge when I remembered – if Beth was going to escape from hospital, I had to bring clothes for her. I thought about bringing the rug, but then remembered how stubborn Beth can be. I was fairly sure I couldn't persuade her to escape if all she had to wear was a woolly rug.

I peeped around the hedge into the garden of Eddie's house – and saw a miracle. There was a washing line full of clothes that I guessed had been out all night. I looked towards the house, but all the curtains were still closed; there was no sign of life.

'You owe me, Beth,' I muttered as I ran up the path to the washing line and grabbed a woman's top, a pair of flared jeans and two spotty socks. Luckily they were only a small bit damp. I was just about to escape when I remembered that Beth didn't have any shoes either. In the corner of the garden was a small shed, and when I pushed the door, it opened with a

loud squeak that nearly gave me a heart attack. The shed was full of boring gardening stuff, but right at the back I found a pair of bright yellow wellies that looked like they might fit Beth. I picked them up and put them into a plastic bag that I found on a shelf, and only had a few dead spiders in it. Then I put the clothes on top. For a minute I felt bad. Maybe my granny had really bad taste, and these were her favourite clothes in the world. Technically, I was stealing them, but this was an emergency, and I told myself that in an emergency, stealing isn't all that bad. Then I headed for the gap in the hedge and set out for the hospital.

* * *

It was breakfast time and people were rushing around with trollies full of lumpy-looking porridge, and toast that was either very pale or very burned. Luckily, no one seemed to notice me as I made my way up to

154

Beth's room. I peeped through the open door, and saw Beth sitting up in bed, drinking a glass of milk. I was just about to walk in when I saw a nurse standing in the corner of the room, writing something on a chart. Neither of them saw me, and I thought maybe it was best to keep it that way until I could figure out what was happening.

The nurse hooked the chart on to the end of the bed, and sat down next to Beth. She didn't look like she was in a hurry to be anywhere else.

'I know we haven't managed to contact your parents yet, Beth,' she said. 'But you must try not to worry.'

'I'll try not to worry too much,' said Beth in a small voice. 'But it's hard. Where could they be? Why aren't they coming to get me?'

'You poor little thing,' said the nurse, patting her hand. I smiled. Beth wants to be a software developer when she grows up, but if that doesn't work out she'd be a great actor. 'I'm sure your parents must be worried sick about you too,' said the nurse. 'Maybe

they heard about the accident and went to the wrong hospital. I bet you they're going to come rushing in here very soon – and won't they be glad to see you all well again?'

Beth sniffed a bit and wiped her eyes.

'But in the meantime we're still trying to phone them,' said the nurse.

That wasn't good news. Presumably Donna and her parents were going to come home at some stage, and if they answered the phone ...?

'This probably won't happen,' said the nurse. 'But if your parents don't come here, and if we can't get them on the phone, well, then we will have to contact the police.'

Beth gasped and this time I knew she wasn't acting. 'The police?' she said.

The nurse patted her hand again. 'Don't you worry, dear. You haven't done anything wrong and you're not in any trouble.'

I wondered about that. Was it wrong to come back

in time? Was it wrong to hang out with your dad and try to change his life, even though he was just a little kid? Beth and I *try* not to tell too many lies, but we definitely hadn't told a whole lot of the truth since we'd arrived in 1975. There's something about time-travelling that makes honesty a bit complicated.

'What will the police do?' asked Beth.

'Well, I'm not an expert on police procedure,' said the nurse, and then she gave a little laugh. 'Most of my knowledge comes from watching *Kojak* on TV. But I expect the first thing the police will do is go to your house – you said you live on Castle Street, didn't you?'

Beth nodded.

'Well, they'll go there and ask a few questions, I would imagine,' said the nurse. 'They'll talk to the neighbours, see if anyone knows where your parents might be.' Suddenly the nurse stood up. 'Time for me to see to my other little patients,' she said as she headed for the door. 'You have a nice rest, Beth, and I'm sure everything will be fine.'

I didn't fancy a chat with this lady who was asking too many hard questions, so I ducked behind a basket of sheets and towels, until she was safely out of the way. Then I stepped into the room and closed the door behind me

'Molly!' said Beth. 'I'm so glad you're here. Were you OK last night? Was it scary on your own? Did you see Eddie? Are you hungry? Did you bring me some clothes?'

I ran over and hugged her. 'I've got loads to tell you,' I said. 'But maybe first we need to—'

'We totally need to get out of here,' she said.

'You're so right, I heard some of the stuff that nurse was saying and I think we might be running out of time.'

Suddenly I remembered why Beth was in hospital in the first place. 'Are you better?' I asked. 'I'm so not helping you to escape if you're still sick.'

She nodded. 'Good as new. A doctor came in earlier and said I'm well enough to go – as soon as my

parents come to collect me.'

'Well, we both know that's never happening,' I said. 'Well, not for forty years or so anyway.'

Suddenly Beth looked scared. 'What if they really call the police? What if the police come here? I can't lie to the police, but I can't tell them the truth either.'

'Look on the bright side,' I said. 'Maybe the police won't come here. Maybe they'll go to Castle Street instead.'

'Where no adult has ever heard of me? Oh, Molly, we're in so much trouble.'

'We've got to get you out of here before the police get involved,' I said. 'And look – I've brought something for you to wear.'

As I said the words, I emptied the plastic bag onto the bed. Beth didn't look happy when she saw my granny's clothes and the dead spiders, but she didn't argue. She jumped out of bed, pulled the clothes on over her nightie, and put on the wellies.

'How do I look?' she asked, giving a twirl.

I tried not to laugh. The top was made of weird shiny pink material, and was a few sizes too big for her. Luckily the jeans had elastic in the waist, so even though they looked disgusting, at least they weren't likely to fall down while we were running away.

'Er, the wellies are cool,' I said. 'You look like you're ready to go to a music festival or something.'

'Thanks – I think. Now have we got a plan?'

'Well, the hardest part will be getting past the desk at the end of the corridor where the nurses sit. The nice nurse was there when I came in, but she didn't seem to notice me.'

'If she notices me I'm dead – you'll have to distract her.'

'How?'

'I don't know, but you need to think of something – and quickly – or else I'll be stuck in this hospital forever.'

I knew she was right. If Beth didn't escape, was I supposed to go back to the present on my own, and

cross my fingers and hope that one day she'd follow me? That would be very awkward – and very lonely.

'OK,' I said. 'I'll go first, and when you see me talking to the nurse, you sneak past.'

'Got it,' said Beth. 'I'll wait for you outside the main door.'

Then I gave her a quick hug and went towards the nurses' station.

* * *

'Hello, dear,' said the nurse when she saw me. 'You must be happy to see that your little friend is better. I just wish we could track down her parents – I simply can't imagine why they aren't answering their phone.'

I could imagine very well why that was, so I just smiled at her.

'Maybe they went to bed very early or something,' I said. 'Or maybe their phone's battery is dead?'

She gave me a funny look, and I guessed that 1975

phones didn't have batteries.

I looked at the clock over her head. 'It's nearly nine o'clock,' I said. 'Soon you can try calling Beth's dad at work.'

In the corner of my eye I could see Beth coming out of the room. When she got to the desk, she ducked down and crawled for a bit, so the nurse couldn't see her, and then she ran for the swinging door, and disappeared down the stairs.

'That's a good idea,' said the nurse. 'And when the police get here, I'll pass it on to them.'

'You've called the police already?' I said, trying not to look scared.

'Just a few minutes ago,' said the nurse, smiling. 'It's for the best. Poor Beth has been very brave, but she needs to be with her family now – and the police will have that sorted out in no time.'

'I guess you're right,' I said backing away from the desk.

Was the corridor soon going to be filled with

policemen?

What was I supposed to say if they started to ask hard questions?

'I've got to go now,' I said to the nurse. 'See you later.'

Then I ran through the swinging doors and down the stairs as if hundreds of policeman were on my trail.

Chapter Fourteen

'Do we actually know where Rico's door is going to be?' asked Beth as we walked towards Castle Street. 'I know it *was* here, but that doesn't mean it's still going to be here, does it?'

It was hard to take her seriously in her shiny shirt and too-big flares, but I wasn't brave enough to say that.

I shook my head. 'It always just – shows up, doesn't it?'

'I guess. I think maybe Rico makes up the rules as he goes along.'

'A bit like your dad on the Saturday Challenge,' I said, ducking as she tried to punch my arm.

'Surely Rico wouldn't let us down,' she said. 'After all, we're practically besties by now.'

We were walking past Eddie's house, and I couldn't

resist looking into the front garden. I wanted to see my cute little dad one more time. The sun was shining, and I could see Stephen, all wrapped up in blankets, sitting on a deckchair. At the other side of the garden, Eddie was kicking a football against a wall, with his back to his brother.

'That's so sad,' I whispered. 'Those two have been apart for so long – now they should be doing stuff together. They should be writing another "Hector" story, or coming up with something new. They should be planning their great writing career, and instead they look like they can't bear to be near each other. Let's get out of here, Beth – I can't look at this anymore.'

'I'd love to pick those two boys up and shake them and make them be friends,' said Beth as we walked away.

'Me too – but I guess friendship doesn't work that way. I'm friends with you because I want to be – not because someone said I have to.'

'You're right. If we weren't best friends before my dad and your mum got together, we'd probably hate each other right now.'

That was a terrible thought, and I hugged her quickly. 'I'm so glad things turned out the way they did,' I said.

'Me too,' she said, hugging me back. 'Me too. Hey, Moll, look!'

We were going round a corner, and I looked up to see a door and the most beautiful words ever written – 'Rico's Store – Emergency Entrance'.

I grabbed Beth's arm. 'Come on,' I said. 'Let's go, before it disappears again.'

We ran through the door, past the warm dark room and seconds later we were standing in Rico's shop, feeling breathless and dizzy. For a minute, I felt like I'd woken up from a dream, and was caught half way between stuff that was happening, and stuff that couldn't possibly have happened – or could it?

Rico looked up, and as usual, he didn't seem sur-

prised to see us.

'Back already?' he asked.

That's one of the things about time-travel that I'll never get used to. Beth and I had spent a day and a night in 1975, but in the present, it was like no time had passed at all.

'Er, yes,' I said. 'Here we are.'

Rico looked at Beth's clothes. 'Hmm,' he said. '1975, I would think. Am I right?'

'Yes,' said Beth. 'You're right – and I'm so not loving the way they dressed back then.'

I wanted to get out of there, and didn't fancy a chat about fashion through the ages with Rico. Then I felt kind of sorry. Because of Rico, Beth and I had had all kinds of adventures. She'd got to spend time with her mum, and we'd changed the life of her Uncle Graham. I hadn't managed to help my dad, but at least I'd learned something about him and his brother. So I smiled at Rico.

'It's very nice of you to let us use your door,' I said.

'Thank you.'

He smiled back, and for the first time ever I didn't feel afraid of him. 'You are very welcome,' he said. 'Goodbye.'

* * *

'So,' said Beth as we walked home. 'That was fun – except for the hospital bit.'

'Agreed,' I said. 'And wait till I tell you what I found in the treehouse last night.'

So I told her all about the Hector stories. Then I told her about the story my dad had written after Stephen got sick.

'That has to be the saddest thing I've ever heard,' said Beth when I was finished. 'The poor little kid.'

'I know,' I said. 'It's like something you'd see in a really sad movie – except it's real. The thing is though, we've learned loads about my dad, and what happened to Pablo, but I'm not sure how we're supposed

168

to fix anything. We know Dad felt like his family was ignoring him, but we couldn't change that in 1975, and we can't change it now either. It's in the past, and the damage has been done.'

'Damage can be fixed though, can't it?'

'I guess – but how?'

'Well there's one thing I still don't get – and it might be important.'

'What's that?'

'It's about Stephen.'

'What about him?'

'You said he's always kind of distant with your dad?'

'Yeah, he is – he's been like that for as long as I can remember.'

'But why? We both know now why your dad was sad, but Stephen was the one who got all the attention and all the toys. His mum and dad fussed over him all the time, and cooked his favourite food, and made him feel special. He didn't lose his precious cat like your dad did. Stephen was sick, and then he got

169

better – big deal. So why did he end up acting all weird with your dad?'

'I have no clue – and no clue how we can find out either. I don't want to go back to 1975 right now – I'm afraid the police might be looking for us.'

'True,' said Beth. 'But we could find out the old-fashioned way. Why don't you just ask Stephen the next time you see him?'

I knew that couldn't be as easy as it sounded, but we were nearly home, so I decided to save the argument for another day.

* * *

Mum was reading when we walked into the kitchen.

'Hi, girls,' she said, without looking up from her book. 'Did you have a nice walk?'

'Yeah,' I said. 'It was—' I stopped talking for a second. 'That song on the radio,' I said then. 'I've heard it somewhere before, but I can't remember

where.'

'I love that song,' said Mum. 'But for some reason it always made your dad feel sad. He'd never tell me why. I used to tease him and say it must have reminded him of an old girlfriend or something.'

Then the chorus came on, and immediately I was back in the treehouse, in 1975, and Dad was cuddling Pablo and singing to him.

Beth looked at me, and I knew she remembered too.

'What's that song called?' she asked.

'"You've Got a Friend",' said Mum.

I could feel tears coming to my eyes. No wonder it made Dad feel sad. He sang it to Pablo, when he thought that he was his only friend in the world. Did he worry that Pablo couldn't understand why he had to be sent away? Did he cry when he thought about Pablo waiting for him to come back and rescue him?

Now Mum put down her book and looked at us properly for the first time. Too late, I remembered

Beth's clothes.

Mum started to laugh. 'Have you been invited to a fancy-dress party, Beth?' she asked.

Beth went red. 'No, Charlotte ... I ... well ... you see what happened was ...' she said.

'We were just messing around,' I said. 'You know – pretending we were—'

And then I remembered. 'Your real clothes,' I said to Beth. 'Where did—?'

'Molly's right,' said Mum. 'Where did you leave your real clothes, Beth? When you went out you looked so lovely.'

And then I remembered the worst part. 'You were wearing *my* jeans!' I said.

'So where are they now?' asked Mum. 'And your nice blue top?'

Mum doesn't usually give Beth a hard time (which drives me crazy), but she's a bit obsessed with us minding our stuff.

'Oh,' said Beth. 'They're—'

Then Mum looked at my hoodie. 'What's that stain?' she said. 'That hoodie was clean this morning. Do you think I have nothing else to do all day besides washing your clothes?'

I looked at my sleeve and saw the dark patch of Beth's blood, but before I could answer, Mum was looking at something on Beth's wrist.

'Is that a *hospital wristband*?' she asked. 'What's going on? What on earth have you two girls been up to today?'

Well, we were trying to fix Dad, so we just went back in time and we hung out with him when he was a little kid, and we saw Stephen when he was really sick and we saw Dad's cat, who was totally cute and now we know why he won't have a cat now and then Beth got knocked down, and she spent the night in hospital and I slept in a treehouse and ...

'Oh, this?' said Beth. 'It's my friendship bracelet. It's new – I only got it ...'

Mum put down her book. 'Girls?' she said, star-

ing at us like she could see right into our brains and figure out what we weren't telling her. I so don't like it when she does that. Even when I haven't done anything wrong, that look of hers makes me feel guilty. Beth pulled a chunk of her hair over her ear, hiding the plaster and the place where the nurse had cut her hair. If Mum ever saw that, she'd lose it completely.

'Mum!' I said. 'You're always telling us to turn off the TV and do imaginative stuff – and that's what we were doing. We thought you'd be happy – instead of treating us like we're criminals.'

'And you were right, Charlotte,' said Beth. 'Being imaginative is so much fun. Beth and I are thinking we might make a Swingball set later.'

Mum didn't look convinced. I knew I had to distract her – and I knew exactly how to do it.

'Didn't you ever play dressing up when you were a little kid?' I asked.

Beth smiled. She's known me for a long time and she knew exactly what I was trying to do.

Mum gave a big sigh. 'I loved to dress up when I was a girl,' she said. 'My sister Mary and I had a whole box of weird and wonderful clothes and accessories. We used to fight over who would wear my mum's wedding dress and we ...'

Beth and I let Mum ramble on for a bit, and then we invented some important homework and went upstairs.

Chapter Fifteen

I found it hard to sleep that night. I couldn't help thinking about my dad, and the cute little kid he'd once been. I realised that knowing about his past wasn't going to solve anything. Finding out why he was sad was one thing, but fixing it was going to be a whole lot harder.

Next day, Beth and I walked home from school together as usual. We were just at our front gate, and I was telling her about the film our science teacher had shown us.

'And first it was like we were watching these really cool, exotic creatures,' I said. 'And they were waving their legs in the air and being really graceful, and then the teacher told us they were head lice, and it was so gross, and Barry screamed and I couldn't stop scratching my head, and ...'

'Hey,' said Beth. 'Isn't that your Uncle Stephen?'

I looked where she was pointing and nodded. Last time I'd seen Stephen, he was a pale, sick little kid lying in a deckchair. Now it was very weird to see this strong, healthy grown-up walking towards us. Stephen is always nice to me, but I *so* didn't want to see him right then.

'You've got to ask him,' said Beth.

'But …'

'You promised.'

'No, I didn't.'

'Whatever. You should have promised anyway.'

'She should have promised what?' said Stephen, stopping beside us.

'Oh,' I said. 'Hi, Stephen. This is my friend, Beth. I forgot to introduce you when we met with my dad before.'

'Hi, Beth. Hi, Molly,' he said. 'How are you two girls today?'

'We're fine,' I said. 'Except we're in a bit of a rush.

We've got so much ...'

Beth kicked me. I glared at her and she glared back. We would probably have had a long glaring competition, except Stephen was giving us funny looks.

'Er, Stephen, actually, there's something I've been wondering about for a while,' I said.

'And what's that?' he asked.

'Well, when you and my dad were kids, did you hang out together?'

'That's a strange question – why haven't you asked your dad this?'

'Well, I sort of tried once, but Dad ... Well it didn't work out. He really didn't want to have that conversation with me.'

Stephen rolled his eyes. 'He never likes talking about hard stuff, does our Eddie.'

That was a bit mean, but I just smiled at Stephen. 'So won't you tell us? Did you and my dad do fun stuff together back in the day?'

Stephen put on that face that Mum does when you

178

ask her about the olden days.

'Oh, yes,' he said. 'Eddie and I were the best of pals when we were little. We had this very cool treehouse in our garden, and we spent a lot of time there.'

'What did you do?' asked Beth, innocently, like she didn't know the answer already.

'Oh, the usual boy stuff, playing with model cars, collecting things – but mostly—'

'Mostly what?' I asked.

'You know, I haven't thought about this for many years,' he said. 'But when Eddie and I were seven or eight, we spent a lot of time writing stories. We came up with this character …'

'Hector the Brave,' said Beth and I together.

'That's right,' said Stephen, 'But how did you …?'

'Lucky guess,' I said. We'd need to be the best guessers in the world to get that one right, but Stephen was so busy remembering his childhood, that he didn't comment.

'Hector the Brave,' he said. 'Our very own super-

hero. Eddie and I planned to become authors when we grew up. We were going to write loads of Hector stories and become millionaires.'

'So why didn't that happen?' I asked.

'It seems foolish now,' said Stephen. 'But there was this horrible boy who lived near us. His name was Billy. He mocked Eddie and me mercilessly.'

'I can imagine how awful that was,' I said. That wasn't hard – in my mind I could see Billy's cheeky face. Mum always says that bullying tells you more about the bully than the victim, and I guess Billy had his own stuff going on. Only thing was, I didn't care about Billy. I only cared about Dad and Stephen.

'Eddie and I were quiet, shy boys,' said Stephen. 'We weren't able to stand up to Billy. He made us believe that writing wasn't cool, so we just stopped doing it. It's frightening how strong peer pressure can be.'

'I totally get why you stopped writing,' I said. 'You were only little kids, and Billy sounds like a brat.

When you and Dad were older though, why didn't you ...?'

Now it was like a shadow passed over Stephen's face. All of a sudden he seemed stiffer and not so friendly anymore.

'You're asking a lot of questions about Eddie and me,' he said. 'What's brought that on?'

For a second I thought of making up a story about a school project on families, but then I stopped myself. Sometimes the truth is the only way to go.

'Sorry if we sounded rude,' I said. 'It's my dad. Since he got back, he's been sad all the time. He hasn't got any friends anymore, and ... well I don't know what to do to help him, but you're his brother so I thought ...'

Stephen sighed. 'Now you're digging up ancient history,' he said. 'Things went wrong between your dad and me a very long time ago,' he said.

'What happened?' I asked.

Stephen looked at me for a long time and I couldn't tell what he was thinking.

Did he want to walk away and end this conversation?

Was he cross with me for being so cheeky?

Was I just wasting my time?

And then Stephen started to talk.

'I was sick for a long time when I was eight or nine,' he said. 'I spent many long months in hospital, and Eddie never came to see me, not even once.'

'But he wasn't allowed!' I didn't mean to say the words, but they popped out all on their own.

'He told you that?' asked Stephen.

'No,' I said. 'I just think that maybe in the olden days kids weren't allowed in hospital – or maybe your parents were afraid my dad would get sick too if he hung around there.'

'I never considered that possibility,' said Stephen. 'I simply thought that Eddie didn't care about me. When my parents visited, they told me all about his daily life, and it sounded like he was having a wonderful time – as if he were too busy to care about me.'

'That must have been tough,' said Beth.

'It was,' said Stephen. 'Things were very difficult for me. I was bored most of the time. I was weak and sick and pretty much confined to bed. Sometimes I was so unwell I could barely walk to the bathroom on my own, and every day I had to lie there and listen to my parents talking about the football matches Eddie was playing, and the birthday parties he was going to. It sounded as if he barely noticed I was gone – as if he was doing perfectly fine without me.'

I looked at Beth. We'd never thought of it like that. We'd been so busy worrying about my dad, we'd never stopped to think what things were like for Stephen. Imagine spending months in hospital without a tablet or a games console to pass the time.

Imagine not being able to message your friends or send them a picture of your dinner.

Imagine thinking that your only brother was having a wonderful life, and couldn't be bothered going to see you.

'And then ...' Stephen stopped talking for a second. It was hard to tell for sure, but I thought his eyes were starting to fill up with tears. 'And then, when I got home after all those months, I was looking forward to seeing Eddie again. I thought things would be just like before – but they weren't. Eddie had grown taller while I was gone. He was almost as tall as me, and he was sturdier too – but that wasn't the biggest change.'

'What was the biggest change?' I asked.

'It was as if my cute and funny kid brother had vanished,' he said. 'The boy I came home to was so cold ... so distant ... I tried to talk to him ... but ... he seemed to be pushing me away.'

'I'm just guessing here,' I said. 'But maybe Eddie was jealous of you?'

'But that doesn't make any sense,' he said. 'I was the one who was sick. Why on earth would he ...?'

'Maybe he felt a bit left out – like you were getting all the attention?' said Beth.

'Did you get presents while you were in hospital?'

I asked, thinking of the big bags of toys Eddie had carried into the house. 'Dad's always going on about how kids nowadays have way more toys than he used to have, so if he didn't have much, and you got loads of stuff, maybe ...'

'I did get a lot of presents,' said Stephen. 'But much of the time I was too sick to play with them – and anyway, playing on your own gets tiresome after a while. Most of the toys stayed in their packages and I was looking forward to sharing with Eddie when I got home, but when I got there he would hardly look at me. I couldn't understand what was going on.'

'Did you talk to your parents about this?' I asked.

'Not much,' said Stephen. 'They worried so much about me, and I didn't want to make things worse for them. Once though, a few days after I came home, my mother saw me crying and asked what had happened. I told her that Eddie wouldn't play with me, and she suggested that I give him one of my toys.'

'That was a good idea,' said Beth.

'I thought so too,' said Stephen. 'I'd have done any-thing to make things right, so I gave him my favour-ite thing – my View-Master.'

'That was kind of you,' I said, even though I had no clue what a View-Master was. 'Did my dad like it?'

'He threw it on the ground and it broke into tiny pieces,' said Stephen. 'And he said something I couldn't understand. He said that a stupid toy would never make up for losing his favourite thing in the whole world.'

'I'm so sorry, Stephen,' I said. 'Sounds like you being sick was a disaster for your relationship, and the whole Pablo thing can't have helped.'

And then Stephen smiled, which was really weird. 'Pablo!' he said. 'Eddie loved that cat so much. He was such a little cutie – it's so sad that we couldn't keep him.'

'I know it was your parents who made the deci-sion,' I said. 'So it wasn't really your fault - but I guess you still felt a bit guilty about it.'

Stephen was looking at me like he had no clue what I was talking about, and too late, I remembered that Eddie was told to make up a story about why Pablo had to go.

Didn't Stephen ever think it was suspicious that Pablo got unmanageable on the exact day he came home from hospital?

Had he never discovered the truth in all those years?

How could one single lie last for so long?

'Why would I feel guilty?' asked Stephen. 'Losing Pablo was nothing to do with me.'

Beth and I looked at each other, and for a minute no one said anything. Then Stephen scratched his head. 'Are you trying to tell me something here, Molly?'

How could I answer that?

I looked at him, and pretended it was one of those stupid questions grown-ups ask, when they already know the answer.

'This all happened so long ago,' said Stephen. 'And I really can't remember the details that clearly. You need to tell me the truth, Molly. Was Pablo sent away because of me? If that's the case ...'

I really didn't want to be the one to break it to him.

'I think you and Dad need to have a talk,' I said.

'Oh,' said Stephen. 'Do you think so? Maybe ... some time, in a week or two, that would be a good idea.'

I smiled. 'I can see why you and my dad were such buddies once upon a time – you're exactly like each other. Didn't you two ever learn that it's good to talk about stuff?'

Stephen didn't say anything, and I wondered if I'd gone too far. I looked desperately at Beth, and luckily she came to my rescue.

'My dad always says that there's no time like the present,' she said. 'Molly and I were just on our way over to see Eddie. Why don't you come along with us, Stephen?'

That was nice of her. We were really supposed to

be going home so she could get started on the big project she had to do for art class.

'Yeah,' I said. 'That's a great idea. You should come.'

For a second I felt sorry for Stephen. I could see he was desperately trying to think of an excuse. Then I stopped feeling guilty – if he and my dad could be friends again, that would be good for everyone, wouldn't it?

'What do you think, Stephen?' I said.

He smiled at us. 'I think you two aren't going to take no for an answer.'

'Yay!' I said. 'Mum might have forgotten that we're going over to Dad's so I'll run in and remind her – and then we can go and have a nice chat with my dad. Don't go anywhere without me!'

Before anyone could argue, I raced inside and told Mum we'd be back in time for tea. Then I ran upstairs and pulled something from my cupboard and shoved it into my school bag. Then I went outside and Stephen, Beth and I set off for my dad's flat.

189

Chapter Sixteen

'**H**ey, girls!' said Dad as he opened the door. 'It's so nice to see you. Have you got time to go for burritos?'

Then, when the door was fully open, he saw Stephen standing next to us. Dad's smile changed, so it looked fake, like he really didn't want to smile at all, but felt he had to, because we were all looking at him.

'Hello, Stephen,' he said. 'To what do I owe this honour?'

I wanted to punch him. This was his brother! Why couldn't he just hug him, and talk about football, the way brothers are supposed to?

Then I remembered that the last time I'd seen my dad, he'd been a lost and lonely little boy.

'Er, Dad,' I said. 'Beth and I bumped into Stephen and we were chatting about the olden days, and ...

well ... you see ... we sort of ...'

Stephen stepped forward. 'I think these two girls want to do a bit of matchmaking between us.'

'Is that right?' said Dad, staring at me in a way that told me he really wasn't very happy.

I stared back at him. I saw his wrinkles, and his glasses, and the places where his hair is getting thin. And then, like magic, I couldn't see those things any-more. For one second, I could see the sad little boy still hidden inside the grown man standing in front of us, and I couldn't hold back anymore.

'Dad, you're so sad,' I said. 'And we want to help you, but we don't know how. When I'm sad, I talk to Beth, and afterwards I feel better and everything makes more sense – and Beth isn't even my sister. And you've got a brother, and you should be the best of friends – and once you were the best of friends – and now you're like two stone statues when you're together – and it's so stupid – and please, Dad, just talk to Stephen – please – and don't just talk about

the weather – talk properly – about real stuff – about important stuff. I want you to do it for me – but mostly you need to do it for you.'

I ran out of breath and waited for Dad to shout at me and tell me to mind my own business – but he didn't do that.

'You're such a lovely girl,' he said, and then he hugged me so hard I thought my ribs were going to crack.

Finally he let me go. 'Maybe you'd better come in.'

We followed Dad into the living room, and we all stood around awkwardly. 'Beth and I could go into the garden and get started on our homework,' I said. 'So you two can have some privacy to say what you need to say.'

'Good idea,' said Dad, even though he looked like I'd suggested the scariest thing in the world. He sat down on the couch, and Stephen sat on a chair at the other side of the room. Dad played with his watch, and Stephen stared at the carpet, like he was trying

to remember the ugly sunflower pattern forever. This was even harder than I'd expected.

'Look,' I said. 'You guys are grown-ups. You can talk about whatever you like, or about nothing at all, if that's what you want. But since you're here, I suggest you at least try to see what went wrong for you both when you were kids.'

They both stared at me, and I wondered if I was wasting my time. Maybe Beth and I could spend a hundred years doing homework in the garden, and still Dad and Eddie wouldn't make things right.

'Pablo.' Beth said one single word and it was like everything in the room changed.

Tears came to my dad's eyes and Stephen twisted his hands together.

'Molly said something about guilt earlier,' he said. 'And I had no idea what she meant. I was still very sick when I came home from hospital, and our parents treated me like I was made of china. They wrapped me up in cotton wool, and protected me

from everything. I know they meant well, but it probably wasn't a good strategy. And now I'm not that sick little boy anymore. Eddie, I know how much you loved that cat, and I know how sad you were when he had to go. Can you please tell me the truth about what happened?'

'Pablo was starting to be troublesome,' said Dad. 'So Mum and Dad decided ...' I felt like shaking him. Had he been telling the lie for so long that he'd actually managed to forget the truth? But then Dad shook his head. 'I was so jealous of you, Stephen.' His voice was quiet, almost a whisper. 'I really believed that Mum and Dad stopped loving me when you got sick. Sometimes I dreamed of getting sick, so they'd love me again.'

'And I was jealous of you,' said Stephen.

'But why?'

'We need to talk about that,' said Stephen. 'And we will – later – but first ... Pablo.'

'That cat was so special to me,' said Dad, wiping

away a tear. 'When you were in hospital, he was my only friend. When Mum and Dad talked endlessly about you, Pablo was the one I told. When Billy was mean to me, Pablo was the one I told. It sounds stupid now, but I talked to that cat. I told him all the things I wanted to say to you.'

'That's not stupid,' said Stephen. 'That's sad – and sweet. I remember that you were a very sweet little boy.'

'When you came home from hospital,' said Dad. 'Mum was terrified that you were going to get sick again, and I think she went a bit crazy. Do you remember how she used to run around the house, cleaning everything with bleach?'

Stephen nodded and smiled. 'I don't know how the bleach fumes didn't finish me off altogether.'

'I was angry at you anyway,' said Dad. 'Because of all the attention you were getting. Then Mum made up her mind that being around Pablo would be bad for you. She said he had too many germs ... she said

he could be carrying all kinds of diseases ... and that's why ... she said ... I had to ....'

Now Stephen had tears in his eyes. 'Oh, Eddie,' he said. 'You mean ...? Pablo had to go because of me? It was all my fault? I never knew about that. No wonder you—'

Beth pulled my arm. 'How about you and I get on with that homework?' she whispered.

So the two of us tiptoed out of the room, and closed the door softly behind us.

* * *

It was getting cold. Our homework was finished, and we'd even studied for the maths test that wasn't going to happen for three more days.

'What could those two be saying for all this time?' asked Beth.

'They've had so many years of not talking properly,' I said. 'So I guess they've got a lot to catch up on.'

'True. But if I starve or freeze to death out here, you and I won't be able to catch up on stuff when we're old, will we?'

I giggled. 'OK, I get the message. It's time for us to break up the brotherly love party.'

As we went back inside, I was half afraid of what I was going to see.

Were Dad and Stephen going to be all awkward again?

Or had Beth and I managed to make things even worse than before?

I opened the door of the living room. Dad was still sitting on the couch, but now Stephen was sitting next to him. They both had red eyes and big smiles on their faces.

'Beth and I need to go home, Dad,' I said. 'I told Mum we'd be back in time to help her make the tea.'

Usually Dad looks sad when I leave his place – even when he knows he's going to see me soon, but now, everything seemed ....different.

'Sure, Molly,' he said. 'I'll see you soon.'

'Oh,' I said, opening my schoolbag. 'I nearly forgot. There's something I want to show you.'

Dad didn't look very excited. I guess he thought I wanted him to sign my homework diary or something.

I pulled out the old exercise book and handed it to him. Stephen leaned over to see too, but in a casual way, like he was just trying to be polite. Dad stared at the cover of the book.

'But—' he said.

'Hector,' said Stephen suddenly. 'It's Hector!'

'Hector the Brave,' said Dad.

'You didn't?' whispered Beth.

'Actually I did,' I whispered back. 'Isn't it great?'

'I can hardly believe my eyes,' said Dad as he turned the cover and looked at the first page.

'This is wonderful,' said Stephen. 'I thought all of these got lost when we moved house.'

'I guess this is the one that got away,' I said.

Dad looked at me. 'Stephen's right,' he said. 'When we moved house, the box of Hector stories got lost. So where exactly did you get this one?'

I could feel my face going red. Beth and I had told Graham about our trips to the past, but we'd agreed that no one else would understand. If we told Dad, he'd tell Mum and Jim, and they'd all gang up on Beth and me. They'd talk about health and safety and they'd find all kinds of reasons for us not to go back to the past anymore. (And they'd conveniently manage to forget about all the people we'd helped by doing exactly that.)

'Oh,' I said. 'I found this story in a box of old stuff – ages ago.'

Dad was still staring at me, and I guessed he was planning to ask some very awkward questions – but then Stephen turned another page and grabbed his arm. 'Look at this, Ed,' he said. 'Remember how Hector fought off the crocodiles? Coming up with that was really quite ingenious of us, don't you think?'

Dad smiled. 'I agree,' he said. 'This isn't bad at all.'

'So maybe you could write more and get them published and we can all be millionaires?' I said.

Dad and Stephen both laughed. That felt so weird, and it took me a second to figure out why – I don't think I'd ever seen those two men laugh together before. I was so happy that I started to laugh too, and Beth joined in, and then we all hugged and everything was wonderful.

* * *

'What if he's angry?' I said a few days later. 'You know my dad, he can be funny about stuff sometimes.'

'If he's angry, we can cancel it,' said Beth. 'But that's not going to happen. He's going to love it – I promise.'

Dad opened the door and smiled at us both. I still wasn't used to how he had changed. In the few days since he'd made up with Stephen, it was like Dad

had got younger and happier. He was almost like a different person.

'Hi, Dad,' I said. 'I know it's not your birthday for another few days, but I've been planning a sort of birthday present for you.'

'That's so nice of you, Mollikins,' he said. 'Are you going to tell me what it is, or is it going to be a surprise?'

'I'd like it to be a surprise,' I said. 'But it can't be really.'

Dad laughed. 'I'm not sure I understand.'

Now that I had to tell him, I felt nervous, like my big idea was really a bit stupid.

'Well, Beth and I saw this poster up in the community centre,' I said. 'And I thought of you - it's for a creative writing course - it's all about how to get started on your first book. It's for writers of kids' books too - we asked - so I've put your name down - and I've paid ten euros as a deposit, but if you think it's a good idea you're going to have to pay the rest

yourself – and that has to be done by this afternoon – or else it'll be too late—'

Dad hugged me. 'You really are the sweetest girl,' he said. 'Have I mentioned that before?'

'So you think the writing course is a good idea?' I asked, feeling hopeful.

'I think it's a brilliant idea,' he said. 'But ...'

I sighed. Why did adults always have to be so sensible? Why did there always have to be a 'but'?

Now Dad was smiling again. 'But you're a day too late,' he said.

'I don't get it,' I said. 'We asked the man. The course doesn't start until—'

'I know,' he said. 'It starts next Monday – and Stephen and I have already signed up. We're going to revive Hector and drag him into the twenty-first century!'

'That's so cool!' I said.

'Thanks,' said Dad. 'We think so too - and to celebrate, how about I take you two girls out for burritos?'

I was starving, but the thought of a burrito ...

Beth kicked me.

'Er, Dad,' I said. 'Beth and I love burritos – well, we *used* to love them, but maybe we could go somewhere else for a change?'

He slapped his forehead. 'I've made you hate burritos,' he said. 'Why didn't you tell me before? Stephen told me about a really nice place that serves all kinds of trendy food – I think you'll love it. Just hang on while I grab my jacket and my keys.'

'Thanks for that, Molly,' said Beth when he ran inside. 'I think you might just have saved my life.'

'You're welcome,' I said.

'Everything's working out perfectly,' she said. 'You should look happier.'

'I *am* happy. It's so brilliant that Dad and Stephen have signed up for the writing course, but ...'

'But what?'

'But now I'll have to come up with another idea for Dad's birthday.'

'Don't worry,' she said. 'There's a few days left, and between the two of us I'm sure we'll think of something.'

Chapter Seventeen

It was the day of Dad's birthday, and Beth and I were walking home from school.

'I promised I'd call over later,' I said. 'And I still haven't got anything for Dad.'

'He'll understand,' said Beth. 'And anyway, he's an adult, so he can just buy his own stuff whenever he wants.'

'Yeah, but presents are different – presents show you care. When Dad was in Africa, I used to post things to him, but half the time they never even made it, or arrived so late he'd forgotten he'd even had a birthday. Now that he's living here again, it's pathetic that I can't find something nice for him.'

'Well, the writing class was a brilliant idea,' she said. 'It's not your fault he'd already thought of it himself.'

'I guess. I just wish I was five again so I could make him a messy card with glitter and glue and wool and stuff and he'd pin it onto the fridge and act like it was the best thing he'd ever seen.'

Beth giggled. 'If you did that now, he'd still have to pretend to love it, wouldn't he?'

'Yeah, but in case you haven't noticed, I'm not five anymore. I'd know the truth.'

'Hey, Moll,' she said. 'I've just had a wonderful idea. Dad and Charlotte don't know that hockey is cancelled, do they?'

'And?'

'And that means we don't have to be home for a bit.'

'So we've got time for present shopping. Thanks Beth, but if I don't know what to buy ...'

'I wasn't thinking of going shopping,' she said. 'Well not exactly, anyway. I was thinking of going to Rico's. I'd like to see 1975 one more time.'

'You're crazy,' I said. 'The police are probably look-

ing for us – well, for you anyway.'

She smiled. 'Maybe they are,' she said. 'But I'm thinking of going back to a time a tiny bit before I escaped from hospital and became Ireland's most wanted person.'

And then I remembered something that had been annoying me ever since we'd come back from the past.

'I get it now,' I said. 'You want to see your mum. I should have said something when we were back in 1975, but I got so caught up with Dad and Stephen and Pablo and ... I'm sorry, Beth, I was being selfish. I didn't think about you at all.'

'You were thinking of your dad,' she said. 'And that so wasn't selfish.'

'Yeah, but ...'

'It's OK,' she said. 'When I was in hospital that night I had plenty of time to think about my mum. She was probably a little kid back then and I'm guessing she was adorable.'

'And you wanted to see her. I get that, and ...'

'I thought about seeing her, but then I changed my mind.'

'I don't understand.'

'Well,' said Beth. 'Seeing my mum might make things really complicated. If I saw my mum in 1975, would she still remember me when she saw me in 1984? How weird would it be if she was nine years older then, but you and I were pretty much the same age?'

'Very weird,' I said. 'But I don't think little kids remember everything, do they?'

'But it's not just that. You see, Moll, I can only remember spending one day with my mum, and that day was so special to me. It was like a precious jewel, that I keep locked away inside me. When I'm feeling sad, I take it out in my mind and examine it. I can remember every single detail of that day. I can remember the sound of the river, and the smell of the food my great-grandmother prepared for us. I can

remember every single word that my mum said. I can remember the way she brushed my hair and laughed at my lame jokes. That day was perfect, Molly, and whenever I think about it, I feel better. No matter what happens to me for the rest of my life, I will always have that special day with my mum. Does that sound stupid?'

I hugged her so she wouldn't see the tears in my eyes. 'No, Beth,' I said. 'That doesn't sound stupid. It sounds very, very smart.'

'Thanks,' she said.

And then I remembered. 'If you don't want to see your mum, then how come you want to ...?'

'Aha!' she said. 'I have a very special plan.'

So Beth told me her plan and to be fair to her, it was an amazing plan.

Come on,' I said when she was finished talking. 'Hurry up. Let's go to Rico's.'

* * *

'Do you ever feel that you've spent too much of your life standing on a footpath, watching old-fashioned cars going by?' asked Beth.

It was ten minutes later (or around forty years earlier), depending on which way you looked at it.

'I feel like everyone's staring at us again,' I said. 'I wish we'd had time to dress up. Maybe you could have worn the clothes I "borrowed" from my granny's house.'

'Oh no, we should have brought them back with us,' she said. 'Your granny might be looking for them.'

'Too late – I think my mum sent them to the charity shop.'

'Speaking of clothes, maybe we could go to the hospital and look for your jeans?'

'No way! The cars and the way people are dressed make me think we're in 1975, but we don't know for sure what date it is. The nurses and the police might still be looking for you, and ...'

'OK, I get it. Maybe that wasn't the best plan in the

210

world. Hey, look who's over there.'

I turned around quickly to see where she was pointing.

How many people did we know in 1975?

And how many of them did we actually want to see again?

I smiled when I looked up the road and saw Donna and Pam on their Chopper. It was lovely to see them, but for a minute I was confused.

Would they know Beth and me?

If we ran over and said their names would they think we were some creepy weirdos?

Beth seemed to be thinking about the same thing, but she was thinking out loud.

'So if they know us, then we know it's *after* our last visit, and if they *don't* know us, then Rico's got it wrong – and that's so not like him. I wonder if ...'

By now the girls and their funny purple bike were beside us.

'Hi, Molly! Hi, Beth!' said Donna.

'Hey,' I said, as I got ready to hug them, before remembering that friends didn't hug in 1975. I took a step backwards and pretended I'd been fixing my hair. Beth giggled, but Donna and Pam didn't say anything. Maybe they were just being polite.

'Donna, Pam,' I said. 'It's so good to see you again.'

It was the truth. I *was* happy to see them. Only problem was, I had no clue what to say next. How could I ask things like, 'Would you mind telling us exactly when it was that Beth and I spent time hanging out in your house? Was that last week? Or a month ago?'

I was all out of ideas, so I looked desperately at Beth.

'So ... er ... what's been happening since we saw you last?' she asked.

Pam gave her a funny look. 'Not much has happened,' she said. 'You only left our house about an hour ago.'

'That's brilliant news,' I said.

'Why?' asked Donna.

Because even though we saw you an hour ago, since then we've been back to our present, and weeks have passed by and my dad is much happier and he's started writing again, but now Beth and I have come back to do one more thing for him, and now, because of what you just said, we know that Rico has landed us in the exact time and place we need to be.

'Oh,' I said. 'It's just brilliant to see you again, that's all.'

For a second Donna and Pam stared at us. I think Beth and I are nice people, but I couldn't blame Donna and Pam for thinking we were very, very weird. But then Donna and Pam both smiled, showing us that they were nice girls too.

'We've got to go,' said Donna. 'We just came down to buy some chocolates for my granny, and Mum and Dad will be waiting for me to get back so we can leave.'

'We'd still like to meet you tomorrow,' said Pam.

'Yeah,' said Donna. 'We could have a lot of fun making that Swingball.'

'And we can go to my place after,' said Pam. 'We've got a Sodastream!'

'Wow,' I said, hoping she wouldn't guess I had no idea what a Sodastream was, and why we should be excited about it.

I really wanted to park all my mixed-up thoughts, and hang out and have fun with our new friends, but I knew that was impossible.

'Thanks,' I said. 'We'd love that too.'

'We still have your number,' said Beth. 'And if there's any way at all to make this work, we'll be in touch again, we promise.'

'Sure thing,' said Donna. 'See ya!'

Then, wobbling a bit at first, our new friends raced off on the coolest bike I'd ever seen.

'I like them,' said Beth. 'I wish we could spend a day hanging out with them, making Swingball.'

'Me too. I wonder what Donna and Pam are like

now – I mean in *our* now.'

'They'll be all grown up. Maybe they've got kids of their own. Maybe they've got amazing jobs they never could have dreamed of.'

'They're going to have such an exciting time. Imagine how surprised they'll be when we get a woman president, and when they learn that women can do anything they want in life.'

'Well, nearly anything,' said Beth. 'I heard my dad say that men are still in charge in most of the big companies all over the world.'

I smiled. 'That's bad – but you and I can work to change that.'

By now, Donna and Pam were at the end of the road. They stopped for a second, waved, and disappeared around a corner.

'Right now we need those two to hurry home so Donna and her family can get going on their visit to her granny's,' I said.

'Why?'

'Because soon some nurses and receptionists from the hospital will be calling Donna's house, expecting your parents to be there. We need that house to be empty.'

'Hey,' said Beth. 'You mean ...? I don't want to get knocked down all over again, Molly. That was not exactly the best day of my life. That cut on my head's just got better and my hair's starting to grow back.'

'And I so don't want to go through another cold and lonely night in Eddie's treehouse.'

But then my brain went all fuzzy. This was very confusing stuff for a thirteen-year-old.

'Does all that stuff have to happen again?' asked Beth.

'I don't know. I hope not. Maybe if you and I just keep away from that quiet country road and don't bump into our other selves, everything will be fine.'

'Good idea. Let's not take any chances. Let's just do what we came here to do, and get back home.'

Chapter Eighteen

'Have you figured out how we're actually going to do this?'

'Not exactly,' said Beth as she started to walk. 'But we know we're arrived at the right time, which is always good.'

'True.'

'And there's some shops over there – maybe Rico's got it right again.'

I followed her and we could see loads of shops selling weird and wonderful old-fashioned stuff. A second later, I smiled as I read the sign over the last shop – Animal Welfare Centre.

'Remind me to get a medal or something for Rico,' said Beth. 'It looks like he's worked his magic again.

'Let's hope we're on time. Let's hope Pablo is still here.'

'But if he is, we still might have a problem. I know it's 1975 and things are different, but I'm guessing they don't just hand cats to random kids who walk in and say they want one. Won't they ask hard questions and want to do a home-check and talk to our parents and stuff?'

'*Now* you think of that?'

'I guess we'll figure it out as we go along, but first, let's go and find Pablo.'

We crossed the road carefully. I wasn't taking any chances so I held Beth's hand like a mum would. She didn't pull away, so I knew she was scared too.

Outside the shop were baskets of bright yellow T-shirts and hats and tea towels, all with the animal welfare logo. A sign next to them read – 'Please buy one and support our good work.'

'Those T-shirts are actually kind of cool,' I said. 'In a 1970s way! I wish we had money to buy one.'

'Me too,' said Beth as she opened the door of the shop. 'But we're looking for a cat, remember?'

I covered my ears to block out the sounds of barking and miaowing and squawking.

The woman behind the counter smiled. 'Don't worry,' she said. 'The animals are like children – they get a bit excited when the door opens. They'll settle down in a minute.'

True enough, it wasn't long before the shop was pretty quiet, except for the gentle chirpy sounds coming from a cage in the corner.

'Well girls,' said the woman. 'Can I help you, or did you just come in for a look around?'

'We're looking for a cat,' I said.

'We always have lots of cats,' said the woman. 'Would you like a grown-up, or a cute little kitten? We have some very sweet black ones.'

'Actually, what we'd like is a grown up cat,' said Beth. 'With grey and black stripes and a white patch under his chin.'

'So you're looking for a tabby,' said the woman. 'We actually have two of those.'

'That's great news,' I said. 'Is one of them a boy, with only three legs?'

The woman gave us a funny look. 'That's rather specific,' she said. 'With strays you generally have to take what you can get – and I'm afraid I've never had a cat exactly like the one you describe. Would you like to take a look at the tabbies we *do* have – even though they all have four legs?'

'No, thanks,' I said. 'We especially wanted a three-legged one – you know – so we could give it extra love.'

The woman shook her head. 'Well, if you change your minds, do come back in, but bring your mammy or daddy with you – you're welcome to look around anytime you like, but we can't actually give animals to unaccompanied children.'

'OK, thanks,' said Beth.

'Well, that was a big success – not!' she said when we were back out on the street.

I hugged her. 'It was a great idea, and it's not your

fault it didn't work out. I'm glad we never got a medal for Rico. Let's get back home before ... well, you know ...'

Beth grabbed my arm. 'Look,' she said. 'I recognize that blue car.'

She was right. Eddie's dad's car stopped right next to us, and reversed into a parking space.

'Ha!' said Beth. 'I knew Rico wouldn't let us down. We're just in time to—'

'But if Pablo goes into the animal welfare shop we won't be able to get him back. You heard what the woman said. If we don't bring some grown-ups with us, we won't be able to—'

'You're right,' she said. 'Oh Molly, I really wanted this to work, and now ...'

Eddie's dad had got out of the car, and was walking around to the back door.

'Quick,' I said, grabbing one of the bright yellow T-shirts. 'Put this on.'

'But—'

221

'There's no time to explain. Just do it.'

Beth didn't argue. She pulled the t-shirt on over her uniform, and I did the same. Then I grabbed a cap for each of us, and we put them on.

'What's the plan?' began Beth. 'What are we—?'

Eddie's dad was beside us now, holding the box with Pablo inside.

'Hello, sir,' I said. 'How can we help you today?'

Next to me Beth stood up straighter, and I knew she knew what I was doing.

Up close, my grandfather was a serious, scary man. Part of me wanted to run away, but I knew I had to be brave, for my dad's sake.

'Can we help you with something?' I asked, trying to stop my voice from shaking.

'You look very young to be working here,' he said.

'Oh, it's a special EU initiative,' said Beth. 'They're trying to get us used to work at an early age.'

'What's the EU?' he asked.

I knew the EU had been around for ages, but I

guess it was called something different back in the day – only trouble was I had no clue what exactly that was.

Then Pablo came to our rescue by miaowing loudly.

'Are you dropping that cat off?' I asked.

'Unfortunately, I am,' he said. 'One of my children is very attached to him, but my other child has been ill, so we don't have a choice in the matter.'

Even though what you're doing is so cruel?

Even though Eddie is still going to be upset in forty years' time?

For a second, I wondered if I could make him change his mind. 'You know cats are very clean creatures?' I said. 'They spend half their lives washing themselves.'

'She's right,' said Beth. 'And did you know that pets make people feel calm – and being calm would help your child to get better quicker.'

'Are you telling me my business?' he asked in a cold voice.

'No,' I said quickly. 'We were just making a suggestion, but we can see now that you've already made up your mind. Why don't you let us take the cat for you?'

I tried not to look too surprised when he actually handed me the box.

'His name is Pablo,' he said. 'He likes warm milk, and chicken, and he's afraid of balloons.'

For a second he looked like he was going to cry, but I guess men weren't supposed to do that in the olden days. Maybe it was hard being a man when you had to pretend to be tough all the time.

'Please do something for me,' he said. 'Please make sure that Pablo goes to a good home.'

'Absolutely,' I said. 'Tell your son that we will find him a wonderful home. Tell him not to be too sad. Tell him that Pablo will always be loved, and—'

'How did you know that my child was a son?'

'Oh,' said Beth quickly. 'I guess there was a fifty-fifty chance – and Molly got it right first go. She's good at guessing.'

He was looking very suspicious, but luckily Pablo miaowed again.

'We'd better get this guy inside,' I said. 'It must be time for his tea. I'll warm the milk, Beth, and you can get that lovely chicken from the fridge.'

My granddad reached out and touched the lid of the box. 'Bye, Pablo,' he said. 'Be good.'

I felt sorry for him. I guess he was just trying to do the right thing, and had no clue how much damage he was doing at the same time.

'Tell Ed— I mean, tell your son that Pablo is going to be fine,' I said. 'We promise.'

'I will,' he said and then he jumped into his car and was gone.

'Great idea, Moll,' said Beth. 'That was really—'

Just then the door of the shop opened and the woman came out.

'Still here, girls?' she said, smiling. I noticed that she was looking at our T-shirts and hats.

'Oh,' I said quickly. 'We were just trying these on.

225

No offence, but we don't love them – yellow really isn't our colour.'

I put the box down on the ground so I could take off the T-shirt, and once again, Pablo gave a loud miaow.

The woman stared at the box. 'Have you got a cat in there? You didn't have that with you a few minutes ago, so where did it come from?'

Answering either of those questions truthfully so wasn't an option. If we had to hand Pablo over ...

'Miaow,' said Beth loudly. 'Miaow. Miaow.'

'She does that sometimes,' I said to the woman. 'It's kind of a protest because her dad won't let her have a cat. It drives him crazy.'

'So if your friend is the one who is making that awful noise, please tell me what is in the box,' said the woman, who wasn't smiling any more.

'Have you ever heard of pet rocks?' I asked.

Now the woman made a face. 'Indeed I have. They are the most ridiculous thing I've ever heard of. Don't

people know how many beautiful living, breathing animals we have here? Don't they see what a waste it is to lavish time and money on a ... stone? And the worst thing is, I'm afraid that foolish fad is never going to end.'

'Oh, I think it will die out eventually,' I said. 'One day there will be a whole lot of kids who've never even heard of pet rocks.'

'I hope you're right,' said the woman. 'Now put those t-shirts and caps back in the basket – and be on your way.'

So we did as she said, then I picked up Pablo and we set off for home.

Chapter Nineteen

'I see you brought a little friend back with you,' said Rico.

The box was still closed and Pablo was being quiet for once, so I had no clue how Rico knew. For a second I felt scared. Was bringing animals back from the past against the rules?

Were there even rules?

What if time travel was dangerous for cats?

What if we did all this and ...?

'Er, is that OK?' asked Beth. 'Bringing a cat back with us? We didn't steal him from a family or anything – we got him in the animal welfare centre.'

'In that case, you did well,' said Rico. 'Not all cats found good homes in the 1970s, so I think you might have done this little guy a favour.'

'So it's really OK? I asked.

Rico smiled. 'Your intentions are good, so it is perfectly fine. And animals adapt more easily than humans do.'

'How do you mean?' asked Beth.

He smiled, and for the first time ever, I understood that Rico wasn't creepy – he was just a bit … different. 'Animals don't fret about time the way humans do,' he said. 'They simply live each day as it comes,' he said. 'I wouldn't recommend bringing an elephant or a rhinoceros back from your travels, but a cat – I think we can allow that. Just don't make a habit of it.'

'Thanks,' I said as we headed for the door. 'Thanks very much, Rico.'

* * *

When we were safely outside, I put the box down on the ground and opened a corner. Pablo's little black face poked out and he licked my finger with his scratchy, sandpapery tongue.

I stroked his ears for a minute and then pushed him gently back inside.

'Sorry, Pabs,' I said. 'We've brought you this far, and we're not going to let you get away now.'

'Come on,' said Beth, picking up the box. 'I can't wait to see your dad's face. He's going to be so surprised.'

She was right. The only thing was, I still couldn't make up my mind if it was going to be a good surprise or a bad one.

* * *

'Happy birthday, Dad!' I said.

'Thank you, darling,' said Dad. 'Have you time to come in for a quick visit?'

'Sure,' I said. 'We have to be home for tea, but that's not for a while.'

Beth and I followed Dad into the kitchen. I couldn't help feeling nervous. Dad got so cross when we tried

to give him one of Graham's kittens, and now – was
he going to go completely crazy?

Beth smiled at me, and I could see that she was
nervous too.

'Er, it's a nice day, isn't it?' I said.

'I thought it was going to rain, and then it didn't,'
said Beth.

It was so lame, but I would happily have talked
about the weather for hours. Only thing was, Beth
was holding a big cardboard box in her arms and I
knew Dad wasn't going to ignore it forever.

'Er, Dad,' I said. 'We've brought you a present. I
know you might be cross when you see what it is,
but, please don't be— please think about keeping it—
please don't—'

'Sorry, Molly,' said Beth, putting the box on the
kitchen counter. 'My hands are killing me.'

'What's in the box, Molly?' asked Dad quietly.

'Er,' I said.

'Er,' said Beth.

'Miaow,' said Pablo.

'Molly,' said Dad. 'I know you're trying to help, but I told you before—'

I started to cry. 'Please, Dad,' I said.

'How many times do I have to tell you? After I lost Pablo—'

'Please, please, just look at him.'

Dad put his arm on my shoulder. 'I'm sorry you're upset, Mollikins,' he said. 'If it makes you feel better, I'll look at the cat, but then it'll have to go back to wherever you got it. OK?'

'We'll bring it back if that's what you want,' said Beth. 'But you have no idea how complicated that's going to be.'

I started to open the box and Pablo popped his head out.

'Oh you little, beauty,' said Dad, stroking Pablo's face.

Pablo purred loudly and then he climbed right out of the box. Dad looked at the white patch under his

232

chin. He looked at the tiny stump where one of his front legs should be. Pablo jumped into his arms and snuggled close, licking my dad's face. He sniffed at Dad's neck, and I wondered if he recognized him. Dad didn't look a whole lot like his eight-year-old self anymore, but maybe that didn't matter to Pablo?

'He likes you,' I said.

'He probably just smells the fish I had for lunch,' said Dad.

Then Pablo slowly raised his paw and patted Dad's cheek three times.

I could hardly breathe. Dad went pale, and his hands began to shake.

'Pablo?' he whispered. 'Pablo?'

And then Dad started to cry. He didn't make any sound, but tears dripped down his face, and onto Pablo's fur. Pablo licked them and wrinkled up his nose at the salty taste. That was funny, but I guess no one felt like laughing. I couldn't think of anything to say, so I rubbed Dad's back and hoped that would do

instead of words.

I looked at Beth and saw that her eyes were full of tears too. If we weren't careful, we were going to end up flooding the kitchen.

Then I looked into the box and saw the raggy old mouse that little Eddie had put into the box. Dad might believe the story we'd prepared about Pablo, but if he saw the exact same toy ...

Beth saw the mouse too. She grabbed it and stuffed it into her pocket, and smiled at me. At least we had one less thing to worry about.

Finally Dad sniffed a bit and used his sleeve to wipe his face.

'I'm sorry, girls,' he said. 'I don't imagine that watching your dad cry is ever much fun.'

'It's OK, Dad,' I said, as Beth and I wiped our own eyes.

'It's just that ... and I know this is crazy ... for a minute there I really believed ... but that's impossible ... it has to be impossible ... and yet ...'

Pablo was stretching his head backwards, and Dad was using two fingers to stroke the soft skin under his chin. Pablo was purring loudly. Dad looked like he had seen a ghost – which kind of made sense.

'This isn't one of the kittens you showed me before,' he said. 'Where did you get him?'

I was ready for that question. 'From animal welfare,' I said. 'You have no idea how many homeless cats there are in this town.'

'It's uncanny how like ...'

And then I couldn't wait any more. 'I know what you said before, but this is different. This is ...will you keep him, Dad? Please say you'll keep him.'

For a second, Dad didn't answer, and then Pablo stretched up his paw and tapped Dad's face again.

'I think Pablo just made the decision for me,' he said.

'So you're keeping him?' I asked.

'And you're going to call him Pablo?' said Beth.

Dad nodded happily, and hugged me. 'Thank you,

sweetheart,' he whispered. 'Thank you so very much.'

* * *

Dad chopped up some chicken and heated a pot of milk for Pablo, while Beth and I made a bed with a cardboard box and an old blanket. Pablo was happily enjoying his favourite dinner when Beth's phone beeped.

'It's my dad,' she said. 'He wants to know why we're not home yet. I'll say we're on our way, OK?'

I nodded. 'Sorry, Dad. Will you and Pablo be all right?'

Dad laughed. 'I think we'll be perfectly fine. Actually, Stephen is coming over with a takeaway later.'

'That's brilliant news,' I said.

Dad smiled. 'Indeed it is,' he said. 'Family is important – as you well know.'

'Yes, Dad,' I said. 'I get the whole important family thing. I'd love to know one thing though.'

'What's that?' he asked.

'Well, I'm guessing that losing Pablo had something to do with your parents?'

'Why do you say that?'

'Well, did it?' I couldn't answer his question, so I asked another one.

'Yes, you're right,' he said. 'It was my parents' decision. They meant well, but ...'

'So did you end up hating them?'

Dad put his arm around me. 'I think I might have hated them that day, but ...'

'But what?'

'Well, the older I get, the more I realise something important. You can see someone's faults, but love them anyway. My parents were far from perfect, but they did the best they could. I loved them and they loved me.'

'That's sweet,' said Beth.

'Oh,' said Dad. 'With all the excitement, I nearly forgot to tell you my good news. Stephen and I had

our first writing class last night.'

'How was it?' asked Beth.

'It was wonderful,' said Dad. 'Really wonderful, and later on, after we eat, Stephen and I are going to do our homework together.'

'Homework!' said Beth. 'Sounds like a lot of fun. Not.'

'Actually it *is* fun,' said Dad. 'Stephen and I can't wait to get started on our Hector story. We've got lots of ideas already.'

'Dad, that's so cool,' I said. 'That's—'

Now my phone beeped. It was a message from Mum with no words – just an angry face.

'We're out of here,' I said. 'Bye, Dad. Bye, Pablo. See you both tomorrow.'

And Beth and I ran home, laughing all the way.